I Don't Like Corn Flakes
or,
Mum's New Spectacles

I Don't Like Corn Flakes
or,
Mum's New Spectacles

John Buster

iUniverse, Inc.
New York   Bloomington

I Don't Like Corn Flakes, or Mum's New Spectacles

iUniverse books may be ordered through booksellers or by contacting:
iUniverse
1663 Liberty Drive
Bloomington, IN 47403
www.iuniverse.com
1-800-Authors (1-800-288-4677)

Because of the dynamic nature of the Internet, any Web addresses or links contained in this book may have changed since publication and may no longer be valid. This is a work of fiction. All of the characters, names, incidents, organizations, and dialogue in this novel are either the products of the author's imagination or are used fictitiously.

ISBN: 978-1-4401-8454-3 (pbk)
ISBN: 978-1-4401-8453-6 (ebk)

Printed in the United States of America
iUniverse rev. date: 12/04/09

Contents

Introduction

This is a collection of short stories about incidents that have occurred during my life. Several contain swear words and words of a sexual nature, and most of them are true.

The exceptions are "The Cruise," which is mainly fiction, and "Don't Wave – We're British," which was told to me by an oppo.

In the story "I Don't Like Corn Flakes," I explain why I didn't like them the way my father dished them up.

Have you ever been frightened by your mother? I loved my mother very much, but when I was a child, she frightened the life out of me, as in "Mum's New Spectacles."

Have you ever yearned for something that you couldn't have? I always fancied a bloater (smoked herring) but never did get the chance to have one when I was young.

Some ladies with whom I have associated have no regard for husbands or boyfriends, so it was not unlikely that the first girlfriend I met sent me a Dear John as soon as I volunteered for the Navy.

This book could (if I wanted) be divided into three sections: before the war, during the war, and post-war.

Mum's New Spectacles

We lived in a small, terraced house consisting of three bedrooms, a front room, a kitchen, and a passage. We had the house to ourselves, as my mum and dad were buying their house, whereas all the adjacent houses in the street were rented. I used to share one bedroom with my sister; it was about twenty feet long by eight feet wide, just enough room to hold two single beds.

When I was about six, I used to sleep in a wooden armchair that folded down into a bed. In those days, the walls were made of lathe and plaster, and they housed all kinds of insects. Before Dad went to bed, he would come into my room and squash the bugs on the wallpaper; they came out at night to feed on one's blood. Invariably he would also lift me up in my half-dopey state and turn me over, saying, "Never sleep on your heart, son." This I could have done without, for I was quite comfortable in my little world.

One night, my mum woke me. Her face was about six inches away from mine, and she was grinning, and it frightened the life out of me. (Now, don't get me wrong – I loved my mum.)

She said, "Can you see anything different in me?"

Well, why should I even bother? I wanted to get back to the Land of Nod. "No," I said.

She said, "I've got a new pair of glasses." *Oh, good,* I thought. *Now let me get back to sleep.*

Many times since then, I have been accused of being unobservant. "Do you notice anything different about me?" a girlfriend would say.

"Well, you've got a few more wrinkles."

"Just like you," would be the reply. "I've got a new hairstyle" or "I've dyed my hair." (They just never appreciated that I preferred it as it was.) Still. I digress.

My birthday was very near to Christmas, so all my aunts would say, "Well, I haven't bought you anything for your birthday, so I'll buy you a bigger present for Christmas."

When Christmas came, I think that they forgot I even existed: I got naught. One Christmas morning, I went round to my cousins' house to see all the wonderful toys that they had got from Father Christmas.

I was quite happy with what I received. I'd gotten a torch, a long balloon, a new shiny penny, an apple, and an orange. With those, I was able to play searchlights and airships for a long while in the dark. My Uncle Ted came in loaded with presents. He had been down to Petticoat Lane that morning, and he handed my four cousins a toy concertina full up with toffees. I didn't get one, but he turned round to my Uncle Harry and said, "I didn't know he'd be here." So I don't think I was very popular.

Anyway, one year my mum bought me a brand-new pair of plimsoles for my birthday. They cost five pence – a fortune. I couldn't wait to get them on, and then whilst she was shopping, I went out into the street and played football with the lads, forgetting that I had my new shoes on. In the rough and tumble that took place with my friends, the uppers came away from the soles. What could I do? I had a flash of inspiration – I'd stick the soles back on. I went indoors and looked for something I could stick them with, but the only sticky thing was a tin of condensed milk in the larder. I liberally applied the condensed milk to my plimsoles, but it didn't half make my socks sticky as well. The aftermath is best forgotten.

I Don't Like Corn Flakes

Mum loved walking, and very often she would drag me along with her (very reluctantly). It was about 1936, and I would have been ten years old. She decided that we would go to Battersea Junction, so we set off along Wandsworth Bridge Road, and on the corner of Wandsworth Bridge was a garage. There was a beautiful white Packard for sale, stated to be the property of George Formby (the famous film star), but it had a cracked cylinder head (whatever that was).

Mum said, "When you grow older, boy, I'll buy you a car like that. Then you can take us all for a ride."

(It never happened, of course, but it was a nice thought.)

The price of the car was five pounds. As Dad only earned two pounds, ten shillings a week (or less), and out of that they were buying their own house, it was a lot of money.

We carried on walking, over the bridge and along Wandsworth's high street until we came to Battersea Market. I loved the smells originating from the various stalls – fish, fresh-baked bread, and in particular the smell of the pie and eel shop with its aroma of parsley liquor – but of course we were far too poor to purchase anything. As it was a Tuesday afternoon, all the minor streets were filled with totters' barrows (these days, I suppose they could be likened to house-clearance or junk men). They'd go round the streets with their barrows shouting out, "Rag and bone!" and folks would come out and give them their discarded belongings. Mum purchased a picture for one penny; it was a picture of St. John's Square in Venice. The painting was lithographed on the inside of the glass, and in various places it had mother-of-pearl that glinted and sparkled in the sunshine. I used to look at it for hours, and it's the only thing I have today to remind me of my mother.

On our way home, a company called Kellogg's was delivering free samples of corn flakes to every house in the vicinity. Mum was ever alert to freebies and told the representative that he had not delivered one to her house (which was true), and after a short argument, she put a small packet of free corn flakes in her shopping basket.

The corn flakes remained in our larder for many weeks, unopened, and as I was only allowed two slices of bread for my tea, on one particular day I felt ravenous, so my attention was drawn to them. I opened the packet and put them in a dish, and then after reading the instructions, I went to the larder to get some sugar.

The old man said, "What are you doing?"

I said, "The instructions say that one should add sugar to them."

"You don't need sugar," said the old man. "They've got sugar on them already. What are you doing now?" said the old man.

"I am going to put milk on them."

"I have to buy milk," he said. "Give them to me."

So I dutifully handed over the dish and its contents, and he put the dish under the water tap and filled it up.

"There you are," he said. "Now eat them."

Why, oh why did all my schoolmates enthuse about corn flakes? I didn't like them one little bit.

Bloaters

I suppose Motor Bert also had something wrong with him, because he loved his motorcar. He would drive up to the corner shop, carefully putting on his handbrake, open the car door, close it again, and go into the shop for his fags. Then, when he came out, he would get in his car, start the engine, and drive away at full speed. The only thing was … he didn't have a car. I offered to clean it for him for two pence, but he wasn't that barmy.

Mr. P had a greengrocer's barrow in the high street and used his passage to store his fruit and vegetables, and another family lived upstairs. Most houses in the street had more than one family living in the same small, terraced house, but we were lucky, because my dad was buying his house (but mustn't let anyone know). The Fyffes banana lorry used to deliver to Mr. P at Tuesday lunchtime, and we normally hung on the back to get a free ride. To stop us, the driver used to accelerate away very fast. But to get a free ride home, I, with others, hung onto the back, and away he went. When his lorry arrived at my house, I thought I would get off.

The next thing I knew I was sitting in a chair indoors by the hob, and my mother crying over me. Why was she crying? What time was it? Was it time to go to school, or had I just come home? Why did my head hurt? My mother tried to stop me, but I stood on a chair to look in the mirror over the mantelpiece. I had the biggest bump on my forehead that I had ever seen, and I'd had a few before.

In those days, you never called a doctor, because that cost money, and you never called an ambulance; there were no phones. But she washed my face and marched me down to the local clinic, about two miles away. My head was pounding; I had an awful headache and had a job to walk. But when we arrived at the clinic, the sister took one look at my nut and boomed, "Take him home, and put him to bed."

Then why, oh why had we walked all the way down there and back? I could have gone to bed in the first place.

It didn't take me long to be up and about again. I suppose we were street urchins, really, and there was nothing to do indoors. Television hadn't been invented; only a few people had a wireless, and they required batteries and accumulators that had to be frequently charged up, and even that cost three halfpence. We had few games, and it was difficult to read anything because we only had gaslight, no electricity.

I met Dad on the way home from work and said, "Dad, got a halfpenny?"

"A halfpenny? I haven't even got enough to buy myself a half ounce of tobacco," he replied.

Oh, well, we could only but try. I never got any pocket money like other kids at school.

Humph lived in the next turning, and I think he had to work and help keep his family, even though he was only about twelve years old. He always had a streaming nose, and yet he would only have trousers and shirt on, even in snow. He had a big paper round and used to go all round the area selling newspapers; he also had a lot of hangers-on, as he was able to give some of his friends a penny for helping him, so this became his gang.

Bernard was a friend of mine; he later became a professional boxer. We used to spar together, and Humph had challenged him to a fight. This was quite normal: we often had to defend ourselves by fighting in the street, and if one didn't fight, then one could be bullied. Anyway, Bern asked me to go with him to make sure there was fair play. Humph's gang would be about thirty strong, and there would be only two of us. So I went with him, and as normally, all the gang formed a circle in which the fight would take place, but before it started, Percy, a seventeen-year-old member of Humph's gang, challenged me to a fight.

Now, I wasn't afraid – me dad had taught me to box – but I explained that I had only come to see fair play. Members of the gang said that I was a coward, so I agreed to fight Percy. Percy took off his overcoat and then his scarf, and then his pullover, and very carefully he rolled up his sleeves and took up the fighting stance in the middle of the ring, with all the gang cheering.

Now, the old man had always said, "Son, always get the first punch in, and hurt them to begin with." So I did – wallop right on the nose. His nose bled profusely, and he ran home to his parents. I heard afterwards that he'd told his folks that a gang of men had hit him (but I was only a ten-year-old boy).

I went back home to tea, and as usual, Dad had his favourite, two bloaters, and I had two slices of bread and dripping (but it did have some salt on it, so it wasn't too bad).

I said to me mum, "Why can't I have a bloater, Mum?"

And she replied, "Because your father has to go out to earn the money to feed us all."

So for years I looked forward to the time when I would be grown up and have bloaters for tea.

Many years later, when I did have a family and I came home to tea, the kids would have bloaters, and I would have bread and dripping. So I would say to my wife, "Why can't I have bloaters?"

She would reply, "Because I have to build up the children's strength and feed their bones and bodies, whereas you are a fully grown strong man, so you don't need them."

Who could argue with that?

Toilet Seat

When I was about eleven years old, I lived in Fulham with no electricity, only gaslight, and an outside loo in the backyard. The loo had no lighting, and as the loo had a fixed seat, my mother and sister were always complaining that the seat was wet, so I had a brilliant idea how to modernise it and help us all. I started a coke round (coke was the cheapest form of heating in those days, only having either open fires or black stoves to do the cooking), and I would carry fifty-six pounds of coke on my back from the gas works and deliver it to neighbours for one penny a time. When I had earned four pence, I was able to buy a pair of hinges, and then I sawed through the fixed timber seat, put timber battens at the back, and fixed on the hinges. Lo and behold, I had brought our old-fashioned loo into the twentieth century, because anyone could now lift the seat and not soil it in the dark. Mother and sister now complained that when they went out in the dark, if someone left the seat up, they fell down the pan, so my father went out with his heavy hammer and some six-inch nails and nailed it down.

So much for progress in this modern age.

Storm Clouds

It was approaching Christmas 1938, and Uncle Titch was having a Christmas party. I would have been thirteen years of age by then. When you went round his house (where I was born), all the passage was lined with crates of beer from the floor to the ceiling. The parties in those days lasted from Christmas night until New Year's Day.

Early in the evening, all the relatives arrived, and everyone went to the local pub. I had to stand outside, as children were not allowed on licensed premises, but I managed to amuse myself somehow with my fertile imagination. Then we headed back to his house, where the music started and everyone, including myself, gave a solo performance. In those days, I could sing and play the piano and piano accordion by ear. Then everyone got up to shuffle, and they called it dancing. Fred's partner (one never mentioned it – in those days, if you weren't married, it wasn't respectable, and I didn't know what it meant anyway) came over to me and pulled me up and told me it was about time I learnt to dance. Now, she was a very large woman, if you know what I mean, and here I was, a young, very shy lad, being pulled hard into a woman's chest. If I could have breathed, I would have blushed.

Anyway, the party lasted for most of the night, and then all the guests went home (all within walking distance, as no one had cars in those days), but as I was very tired, I was allowed to stay and sleep on the settee.

I woke up, and as the place was a shambles, I cleared and washed the glasses and plates, cleared the open fireplace of ashes, and took Uncle and Aunt up a cup of tea in bed. To my utter amazement, my uncle gave me a handful of custard creams. I was in heaven – I'd never been treated so well – so I scraped all the cream out from inside the biscuits and made a big pile of it, and then I ate the biscuits and left the pile of cream till last. It was very cold, and I noticed that my uncle had his pants and shirt on in bed, but that was nothing unusual in those days, because all the men wore their shirts in bed, and anyway they always changed them once a week, so they were very clean.

That evening, all the relatives gathered in the front room. Uncle had a great big, modern radiogram, and very few people could boast about having one of those. He was able to twiddle the knobs and get foreign stations, and that in itself was amazing. The dark clouds of war were looming, and my dad was an authority; he'd been all over the world in World War I and had fought in the trenches in France and Belgium. No one could speak any foreign languages, but the set was tuned into a station where it sounded like German, and one person would announce to the others, "There you are, he said war," or "There, he said Hitler."

Everybody was wondering if there would be a war or not. It didn't worry me; I was to be seen and not heard, and I'd gotten a glass of lemonade and a sandwich, so I felt like royalty. The party carried on over Christmas, and on New Year's Day after twelve o'clock, we all went out in the street, knocking on neighbours' doors and shouting Happy New Year to all and sundry.

Around April or May, all the schools shut down, and preparations were made to evacuate all the schoolchildren away from London. I didn't want to go; I wanted to stay with my parents, and they said it was up to me what I did. I didn't worry, but I wasn't too happy when Bill over the road (who had also fought in World War I with Dad) said that if one German plane got through our defences and dropped a bomb, then half of London would be destroyed. Rumours were flying thick and fast.

War Breaks Out

As the schools had been evacuated, the ARP wardens took them over, so I used to help fill all the sandbags that were used to put round the warden's office for protection. Across the road were the repair shops of the gas light and coke company, where we would ask them if they had any old ball bearings. We used to build our own toys in those days, and with the bearings, we could build our scooters from two old lengths of wood and a block.

I now remember Chamberlain coming back from Berlin, where he had been talking to Hitler, saying, "This bit of paper means peace in our time."

Sadly, it was not true. Soon after, war was declared. We stood on the doorstep on that Sunday morning, as all the neighbours did, and at eleven o'clock, the sirens wailed their warning.

Make no bones about it, I was scared. As the old fellow over the road had said, it would only take one plane to get through, and half of London would be blown up. I said to my mum, "I wish I had been evacuated now."

She said to me, "Well, it's too bloody late now. You will have to stay here with me."

A couple of months later, I was fourteen, so my mother took me to County Hall to get a school leaving certificate (I was supposed to stay at school until I was seventeen). I found a job in Sloane Square as a petrol pump assistant. I earned ten shillings a week and stayed there for about twelve months, and then I got a job at Cadbury Hall, as a messenger boy. I remember being in the café on the top floor and playing draughts when an air raid warning sounded, and everyone went downstairs to the air raid shelter. A mate and I stayed put, playing our game, and a few bombs dropped and the whole building shook, but still we played on. I seemed to have no fear in those days.

My mother took us all to my cousin's house at night to get away from the constant bombs that were falling every night. Being in Isleworth didn't matter too much, as I am certain that Hitler used to bomb wherever Mother went, and bombs rained down on us. I used to go to work in Hammersmith on my bike, and every morning I was diverted by either an enemy airplane that had been brought down or a land mine that destroyed whole areas of houses.

I used to get behind buses or any large vehicle that could shield the wind off my body to make me go faster, as I had the impression that I was very fast on my Bowen racing bike. One day, coming home from work, I got behind an open-backed army lorry and followed this for many miles. It wasn't until we came to Fulham Broadway that the lorry turned left, toward Chelsea, and as there were stoplights that were red, it slowed down. I went flying past it and had a look in the back of the vehicle, and I saw that it was full up with the biggest time bombs that I had ever seen.

About that time, the council built brick air raid shelters in the streets, but I never used them. I used to go to bed as usual in my parents' small, terraced house and listen to the shrapnel bounce off the roof, because there were constant air raids during that period. My sister, Dolly, used to come upstairs and pull me out of bed, saying that Mum and Dad had gone over to the shelter and they wanted me to join them. I used to say, "Okay, Dolly, I'll get dressed," and then as soon as I heard the front door close, I would crawl back into bed and soon be fast asleep.

At work, my boss decided that I should get a trade, and he sent me for an interview to get an electrician's mate's job. I was transferred to Rannoch Road Jam Factory, where I became an electrician's mate. As the German planes were still bombing London, I started doing my turn as firewatcher, both at work and at home.

I had to do one night a week at work, for which I was paid one pound. One night, being on shift with about ten other men, I was walking round the site when I discovered that an incendiary bomb had dropped on a barge and set it alight. I ran to where all the other men were and shouted out, "There's a barge of jam alight on the wharf!" The men shouted at me to push off because they had been caught like that before, and they just wouldn't believe me. I finally convinced them that I was telling the truth, and the difference that it made was hard to believe. As an efficient, trained, organised body, they went to work and soon had the blaze under control, finally putting the fire out completely. Soon the fire brigade arrived, inspected the fire location, and then, to my amazement, knocked a hole in the bottom of the barge to sink it. They had to do that to make sure that there was no reoccurrence. Anyway, I was later asked by the management if I had damaged any clothing, and I got a pound to purchase some new trousers, except I didn't have any clothing coupons.

One day (during the war), we had a load of strawberries come in. (One never saw them in Civvy Street, and so they were gold dust.) Everyone wanted to get some home for their families, but they sent the police to the factory. One bloke I knew was completely bald and always wore a dirty bill cap. As he was going home, the gate police called him in and told him to strip naked, but they never found a thing. The following morning, he told me that he had taken some strawberries home for his family.

I said, "But I saw them strip all the clothes off of you."

He said, "Yep, but I kept me hat on all the time, and the strawberries were under me hat."

Dear John

For Whom the Bell Tolls was on television this afternoon. I remember; I remember.

It must have been about 1942. I stood in a queue outside the Odeon Leicester Square with the most beautiful girl in the world; she had long blonde hair, a beautiful face, and a figure any girl would be proud to own. She was my dream girl and my first love. She was much more experienced than I was and probably a bit older, but it didn't matter, as I was totally infatuated. At that time, I was completely ignorant of the opposite sex; I didn't know a thing about them, and I didn't even know that there were any differences between boy and girl. We were never taught about sex at school, and my dad said that babies came from under gooseberry bushes, and it didn't enter my mind to think otherwise. When we went to the cinema, she would unbutton her blouse and place my hand on her voluptuous breasts (she never wore a bra), and I was in heaven.

On the way home, we sat upstairs at the back of a bus, and we both fell asleep. It wasn't until the bus had been stationary for some time when we woke up and found we were in the bus garage. It was now so late that we would have to walk the rest of the way home, and there was Jerry dropping his bombs all over the place again. As usual, I escorted her home. She was afraid of the air raids, but it would mean a six-mile walk for me. Passing down a back street in Fulham, we saw a row of houses that were on fire, either from incendiary bombs or an oil bomb. The fire service, ARP wardens, rescue, and police were all doing the best they could, as usual, whilst all the neighbours were crowding round to watch. All of a sudden, there was a terrific explosion; the houses must have also had a time bomb dropped on them. There were people lying all over the place, dead, wounded, crying, screaming, but as there were many ambulances and crews in attendance, there wasn't much we could do to assist, so we carried on walking home. Even though the raid was still taking place, it was heaven saying good night to her on her doorstep, kissing her and pressing up close to her.

We had met at a dance hall near Putney Bridge. She was a good dancer, but it was ecstasy to hold her in my arms. I had intended to go to the Putney Dance Hall over the milk bar, but it was a good job I had changed my mind, because that night the dance hall had received a direct hit, and both the dance hall and the milk bar were crowded. They used the Gaumont Cinema as a mortuary for all the hundred or so young folk that had been killed. During the raid, a few of us stood in the doorway of the hall, watching Jerry fly over, dropping his bombs. The doorkeeper was trying to shepherd us back into the hall, at the same time saying, "Get under cover! You don't know what those bastards can do. I was in the first world war, so I've seen it all."

I glanced at a pilot officer's chest, and in the glow of the fires, I noticed that he was wearing the VC, but he said naught.

I took my girlfriend home to tea to see my parents, and they liked her a lot. Was I a proud boy walking down the street with her on my arm! She told me that she went to night school and was escorted by a married man, also that she had had many other boyfriends, but it all fell on deaf ears because I was so infatuated. As I only saw her once a week, I was getting a bit lonely. All my friends were disappearing.

It was the normal thing now to build air raid shelters in the streets for those folk that didn't have an Anderson shelter in their back garden. These were made with walls of brick and a one-foot-thick reinforced concrete roof, and one of them had been built in the forecourt of the block of council flats in the next turning. One night, a bomb dropped nearby, and the brick walls were blown away by the blast, and then the reinforced roof fell on the people taking shelter, killing most of them (including some more of my friends).

I was now seventeen, and the old man had always said to me, "Never volunteer for anything, son."

So, disregarding his statement, I made my way to Acton Town Hall to join the army. I had always been interested in electrics, so I thought I would join the REMEs. First was a medical to see if one was fit; the place was crowded with young men. We were all sitting on the floor, waiting our turn, when a major came out of a side room and wanted to cross the floor. He said to us, "Oh, mind your tootsies, young men."

Christ, what kind of an army was he in? But I soon found out it was different once you were in. I passed the medical (which was a surprise because as a kid, I'd had a weak heart), I got dressed, and then I went into the army recruitment office.

"Yes, son," said the sergeant major, "what can I do for you?"

"Please, sir," said I, "I want to join the REMEs."

"Sorry," he replied, "the REMEs are full up. Are you over six feet tall?"

"Yes, sir."

"Then I'll sign you on for twelve years in the Irish guards."

"You bloody well won't," I replied.

Next I went to the RAF, which was situated in an adjacent room off the main hall, but they only had flight engineer vacancies, and that involved twelve months studying in Canada, which would have bored me stiff. Next I went to the Navy in the next room; they promised nothing because one could only specialise once one had joined. So I enrolled as an ordinary seaman.

Soon my call-up papers arrived, and I was to report to Skegness aboard HMS *Royal Arthur*. Where the hell was that? The farthest I'd ever been away from home was Southend-on-Mud, or Folkestone. My old man must have known that I had volunteered. He said to my mum, "Well, I was expecting it, but he's a bit young. They don't call them up till they're eighteen."

My folks had a party for me before I left, but my girlfriend didn't come, because she had something more important to do. I had bought her a brooch that cost me six pounds – a fortune in anyone's eyes.

We sat up all night, then I said my goodbyes to everyone and headed off to the railway station. The journey from London to Skeggie took seventeen hours, as the train kept stopping due to air raids. I didn't know that HMS *Royal Arthur* had been a Butlins holiday camp in peacetime, but during the few weeks I was there, I learnt some interesting things, like how to escape from a submarine by wearing an apron when you're forty feet below the surface so as to stop yourself from popping up out of the water like a cork; also how to row at full speed in a boating lake when the oars have holes in them and the dinghy is tied to the side so you have to row like a madman to get nowhere; also how to march on a skating rink.

We had to do fire watching on the roof of the gigantic mess hall. A bomb fell in one of the rows of huts and killed a few men, but that was what I had joined up for. Also, the sea came over the boundary wall, and we had to walk through a few feet of water – so what? The main thing was that standing up there in the winter, it was freezing cold, and the new blue overcoats supplied didn't keep the cold out.

After absorbing all this knowledge, I was off to Malvern Hills for six weeks' square bashing to pass out as an ordinary seaman. During this time, I had heard no word from my girlfriend, so I wrote to her explaining what had been happening and saying that I hoped that she'd wait for me until I returned. To my delight, I received a reply from her, but I wasn't delighted when I read what she had written.

"Dear John, I am not exclusively yours."

I ignored the old man's advice again and volunteered for active service. The most attractive young Wren psychologist I had ever seen in my life interviewed me. (Had she told me that I had to jump out of an airplane without a parachute, I would have done it.) She explained that there were only two things open for me, either of which I would have to volunteer for. The first was being a torpedo man on submarines (I was too good a swimmer to entertain this), and the second was to volunteer as a wireman in combined operations. Now, I had never heard of combined operations, but it sounded better than dying under the water, so I nodded my head. As an ordinary seaman, my base would have been Chatham, and I would be able to get home every weekend, but now that I had joined combined operations, it was changed to Guz, or Devonport, to the uninitiated. When I got there, the base had been designed to hold twenty thousand, but now there were a quarter of a million personnel waiting for draught chits.

I soon grew up to be a man.

Girls' Training Corps, W/C

My next draft was to Malvern Hills, where we had to learn square bashing. After one arduous day, we had a dance in the evening. I got on particularly well with a Wren, so I escorted her back to her billet. We were smooching in a dark corner, kissing and cuddling, when she suddenly lifted up her skirt and said to me, "Do you like my knickers? I knitted them myself."

This put me right off, so I returned to my quarters.

I did six weeks' square bashing, and after passing out, I was given a chit to go to Letchworth. With my tickets and draft chitty in hand, I was off.

I was shown where I would be staying for the next weeks; it was a government training centre, housing about thirty matelots and two hundred ladies who were learning about the maintenance of aero engines.

I had to write to me mum and let her know I was okay, but I didn't like my new address in print. Now, during the war they had created a Girls' Training Corps so that young ladies could get experience to join the Air Force as WRAFs. I was now a wireman candidate, so I was a bit embarrassed when writing my address as GTC Letchworth W/C.

I studied very hard during the day, and then for a bit of relaxation at nights, we would adjourn to the recreation ground opposite the centre. Whilst sitting on the children's swings, we would swap yarns. The new recruits were very anxious to learn about their future.

Bermuda would also tell us about his latest conquest. Everywhere he went, he got engaged to some girl or another, and he always bought them an engagement ring. He must have been loaded; with us earning ten shillings a week, we would have had to save forever and a day to buy one engagement ring. With the number he bought, if they were linked together, they would have stretched from these islands to the West Indies.

I learnt how to get the blue out of my collars and crumple my hats and blues so that it was not so obvious that I had just joined up. Whilst I was sitting on a children's swing late one night, the usherette from the local cinema came through the recreation ground on her way home. Seeing us, she came over to me and told me she wanted a swing. She then sat on my lap and proceeded to swing us backwards and forwards till we were flying quite high, and then she held onto me like grim death. I didn't like to tell her that she had made it quite hard for herself. She jumped off, gave me a smacker on the lips, and was off before I could recover. (Why did they keep on doing that?)

One morning I overslept and was very late reporting in. The regulating officer put me on a charge, and I had to appear in front of the officer of the day as a defaulter. I had to run at the double and then "caps off" in front of the officer. To my surprise, it was a one-legged captain that I saw, and he had been decorated in the field. He asked me what was my excuse, so I told him that normally I was first up and I woke all the other lads, but this morning my alarm clock had failed to function, and all the other lads, thinking I was already up, didn't bother to look for me. He looked down at the papers in front of him, hiding his face, which had a big grin on it, and sentenced me to seven days' loss of shore leave. Seven days' loss didn't matter; there were a load of beautiful birds billeted on the site anyway, and it was a pleasure. Anyway, we all knew that in Kate Carnie's army (combined operations), one was never punished for what one did, only for what one was found out to have done. Our motto was, "Don't get caught."

At weekends we were free, so George and I used to walk as far as the A1 and hitch a lift back to the Smoke. The car and lorry drivers were so kind to servicemen and would stop readily. It was embarrassing sometimes; not only would they give us a lift, but when they stopped for breakfast at a café, they would not allow us to pay (not that we could), and they bought us a full breakfast even though we protested. Then when they dropped us in the East End, they would take us to their local and they and their mates would fill us up with beer and even offer us the fare for the Underground. It seemed they could never do enough for the boys in blue – or in blue and khaki, as far as we were concerned. Often on a bus or train, one would hear a child say to its mother, "Is that man a soldier or a sailor, Mum?"

I had been issued a weekend ration card, so I queued up outside the baker's for bread. Whilst I was in the queue, there was an almighty bang, and a pall of smoke appeared somewhere over Battersea or Wimbledon.

"What was that?" I asked an adjacent person.

"Oh, nothing to worry about," was the reply. "It's only a German V2."

So one minute you could be there, and the next you could go up in a cloud of smoke, but it was nothing to worry about. (The devastation that those rockets caused was unbelievable: whole areas were demolished in the flick of an eyelid.) It was all a matter of luck, I suppose; unlike the Blitz, one could not shelter from these.

Later I went to a little shop in North End Road called Sainsbury's to get my one ounce of butter, two ounces of cheese, and two ounces of sugar. Whilst I was in the queue, it was announced that – wonder of wonders! – the shop had had a delivery of eggs, one per person.

When I got to the counter, all the housewives gave me their rations; I was most embarrassed and told them that in the forces, we were much better fed than they. They insisted on foisting their precious rations onto me.

"Go on, Jack," they said. "You deserve them more than us."

So I went home loaded with eggs, cheese, butter, etc., courtesy of London housewives. I was amazed. I knew that they and their kinfolk were almost starving.

At the end of the training period, I was given a chit to report to my mobile unit.

Fishing Vessel Crew

Roll on the Nelson, Rodney, Renown

These flat-bottom bastards are getting us down

That reminds me ("Here we go again," he said) of the time I got a draft chitty after volunteering for combined ops.

I got a draft chitty to Poole Harbour. After spending one night at the Poole base, I was told to report to Holton Heath, where I was assigned to my quarters. When I saw the craft, I blinked and rubbed my eyes. It was a fishing vessel. I was to carry out duties repairing all types of landing craft, as a member of a mobile unit.

There were eight crew members, all occupying living accommodation measuring eight feet by twelve, including eight bunks and a mess room table. The crewmembers were Hoppy (who thought he was Joe Louis and wanted to fight everyone), Lofty (who was six foot six and broad as a barn door, but if he had contracted a brain tumour, he would have died because the surgeon never would have found his brain), and Curly (who had a metal plate in his head where no hair would ever grow again). Our normal dress was sea boots, working trousers, and navy blue jerseys … oh, and a knife in one boot. I soon learnt not to sit at the mess deck table with a wooden bulkhead behind me, as the lads liked to practice their knife throwing.

We were nowhere near civilisation, but we found that if we walked about five miles along a railway track, there was a nice little country pub. I occupied a top bunk, where after a nice Sunday pork lunch, I could lie down and through the hatch see an eighty-foot mast swaying from side to side. By now, though, there was about four inches of snow on deck, and it was freezing cold. So we "borrowed" a stove, chimney, and fuel and installed it in our mess room. The object now was to see if we could make it glow white hot, but as Lofty suffered from claustrophobia and also went mad on the full moon, he didn't want the place too warm. So after he had had a night supping beer at the local, he used to come back when we were all asleep and piss on it to put it out. The smell in our quarters was beyond belief.

It was Christmas Eve, and seven of us had had a good time at the local, but we had lost Lofty. We all returned to our craft and had crashed our swedes by one o'clock. At about three in the morning, we were woken by Lofty, who had a false grin on his face and was nissed as a pewt. He kept shaking Hoppy, saying, "Want to buy a raffle ticket for a battleship, Hoppy."

"Get your head down, Lofty," came the dozy reply.

"Want to have a piss?" Lofty said to Hoppy.

"Get your bloody head down, Lofty."

This continued for quite a while until Lofty flopped on his bottom bunk under Hoppy. There was peace at last, and we all went to sleep. It must have been about four o'clock in the morning when all of us were woken by hollering and shouting. When we put the light on, there was Hoppy standing over Lofty, pissing all over him, saying, "I didn't want one when you asked me, but I sure do want one now."

The following morning, Lofty's blankets and gear were laid out all over the place to dry, and we all had a stinking Christmas day.

Do you know that after being with the scum of the earth for so long, it has taken me sixty-five years of very high polishing to become the rough diamond that I am today?

Shore Leave

We had lived on this free French fishing vessel for over six months, minding our own business and doing, in the main, what we were told. I think we had all become a bit barmy. There was Lofty, who seemed to be affected by the full moon; Hoppy, who always considered himself to be the best fighter in the mobile unit; Brommy, who was girl crazy (to put it politely) and whose hobby was putting his clenched fist through pub plate-glass windows when they wouldn't serve him another pint. There were Scouse and Geordie, who, no matter where they were, always pulled the knives out of their sea boots and thought it great fun to throw them at anyone at any time, just missing one's ear and then boasting about their skill.

We had just pulled into a jetty on the far side of Poole Harbour, and there was quite a bit of sea mist about; however, as we hadn't had a spell of leave or the taste of a big town for some months and we were only a few miles from Bournemouth (where the matelots had to go around in pairs for fear of being raped by the local girls), we decided we should go ashore. Unfortunately, by now quite a fog had developed, and all the trot boats to the Poole jetty had been withdrawn. Alongside us was a landing craft tank, and we noticed that the skipper had a very nice rowboat on the well deck, and it was not beyond our capabilities to commandeer it.

We set out in our rowboat, and as it was only designed to carry four, we had to sit round the gunwales; as a consequence, we all got wet bottoms to start with. It was rather difficult for us to row the thing; it was not far by trot boat but a very long haul rowing. We got even wetter when we had to change oarsmen, and the journey was made even longer when you consider that it was a winter night with thick fog, and during wartime nobody hung out landing lights to let one know where one was. We considered that we might be preempting the called-for invasion of France (or second front, as it was known to the communists) by a couple of months, but I don't think Jerry would have been too frightened by six matelots in their tiddly suits.

By luck more than judgement we hit a beach and jettisoned the rowing boat, which by now was half full of seawater, and as we had been bailing it out with our caps, I suppose you could say we were a wet lot. Before setting out, we decided to see how much cash we had amongst the six of us, and to our amazement, we possessed one shilling and fourpence (about 6p, Grandson). We considered this an ample sum to have a good night ashore, but we didn't have enough for the train fare from Poole to Bournemouth for one, let alone six. Still, that was no problem; we picked up the railway lines shortly afterwards, and with a couple of miles' walk, we found ourselves on the platform at Poole.

The train journey was uneventful, but there was a problem at the ticket gate, as four ten-foot tall military policemen were talking to the guard. However, there was another matelot who was going on ten days' leave (lucky sprog), carrying a green petty officer's suitcase, and he didn't have a ticket either. We made a grab for a large four-wheeled platform trolley, loaded the suitcase and seven caps onto it, and with about ten servicemen pushing it, we shouted out to the porter, "Draft party coming through!"

The porter duly unlocked the padlock, and the military police pulled open the double gates for us, and we in turn pushed the trolley through and bade them a sailor's farewell.

It was obvious that to have a good time on one and fourpence between six of us, we had to choose the most expensive and best hotel in town, which we duly selected and bestowed with our custom. It was the early days of the Americans' arrival, and the bar was full of them, each having two or three girls in attendance. The biggest trouble in the bars those days was that there were insufficient glasses to go round, and the landlords invariably couldn't bother to serve British servicemen with a pint, as it was much more lucrative to serve an American with shorts. So the only thing to do was to collect all the glasses in the bar and put them on our table.

Shortly afterwards, an American came up and said, "Excuse me, lads, but I can't get a drink, as there don't seem to be any glasses around. Could I have a couple of yours?" We said certainly, and a minute later, a barmaid brought over two pints, compliments of our new friend. We shared one pint between the six of us and returned the American's pint back to him to have one with us. Later he came over to our table and thanked us profusely for our generosity. Saying that he didn't have time to buy his round, as he had to meet his girl, he promptly put three quid on the table to buy ourselves a drink. Christ, that equalled two weeks' pay including hard layers – nice bloke, this American.

Meanwhile, of course, Brommy was chatting up a bird in an expensive fur coat, and as she was on holiday from the Smoke, she promptly bought us all a drink. I was talking to a Canadian flying officer, telling him that if he flew towards a craft, not to get the sun behind him or we were bound to open fire on him. He was a very charming man, and he stood us a round. We did protest at all these people buying us drinks and not allowing us to stand our round, but it was no good. Perhaps it was the water dripping off our bellbottoms onto the carpet that made them keep the beer flowing, just out of curiosity, to see if we also had holes in our guts.

We soon had all the people in the bar singing, and even at closing time we still had several pints standing on our table. We all left the hotel three sheets to the wind and went to the town hall, where we understood there was a good dance on. We walked in single file past the ticket collector on the door, each in turn saying that the tickets were coming on behind. Five of us got through, but Hoppy was having an argument with two men about tickets of some sort. We all went back to the men on the door and explained most patiently that when we went out during the interval, somehow they had forgotten to give us tickets to come back in. We produced our cloakroom ticket, on which we had parked six caps on the one ticket at a total cost of two pence (the first we'd spent tonight), and the doorman apologised to us, and we walked on to the dance floor.

It was a good dance with an excellent band and soloist. All round the hall, there were bunches of flowers in vases; we found out afterwards that it was called a flower dance. Although the band played waltzes and foxtrots, I was "Brahms and Liszt," and for every pretty girl that danced past me, I pulled a flower out of one of the vases and put it in her hair. Soon I had run out of flowers; also, I didn't know that the flowers were to be presented as spot prizes. The organisers and the recipients of the bunches of stalks didn't seem to have any sense of humour.

We had a good night. A few further things happened, which I don't think I'll mention, as I'd be giving away military secrets, about which the authorities have been trying to find out "who done it" for years. Back on the fishing vessel at three o'clock in the morning, we always kept the coke stove glowing red hot to keep us warm in our sleeping cabin, which was about eight by twelve feet in size. It must have been a full moon, although with the fog, I hadn't seen it, because Lofty had another turn. He was now punching the deck head and bulkhead, trying to let more air in. He obviously thought that opening the hatch was too difficult. He finally finished up peeing all over the red-hot stove, and the smell was atrocious, so we opened the hatch for him. We all got our heads down and crashed our swedes, but not Lofty, who went through his normal "happy matelot" routine, shaking Hoppy on the top bunk, and asking him, "Want to have a pee? Want to go in a raffle for a battleship?"

"Get your head down, Lofty," we all moaned.

The following day was clearer, but as we had become a bit bored, to relieve the monotony, we threw various tins and bottles into the Ogin, and with our .22s, we had a bit of practice. We didn't know – until we spotted a white flag being waved from the shore – that our ricocheting bullets had pinned down an anti-aircraft battalion, and they had surrendered to us. I think we should have gotten a medal or something: the only boys in the combined ops to capture a British ack-ack battalion.

Promotion to Leading Seaman

After six months of repairing landing craft, I had to return to Guz (Devonport), and I got another draft chitty to HMS *Raleigh* to take a "Power of Command" course to enhance my chances for promotion to hooky status. We had to sit for ages in a trot boat to go over from Guz to Raleigh, and all the while the shite hawks kept bombing us until our blues and titfers were white. We arrived at Raleigh, and the instructors soon let us know who the governors were. In fact, when they bellowed "One!" we jumped up in the air, and on the command "Two!" we came down again. We were shown where our billets were, and straight away we were on parade (just to smarten us up a bit).

We did lots of marching and PT, and we were allowed two minutes to change from PT kit to our uniforms. All the orders were reversed, so if the instructors said, "Right turn!" we turned left; if he said, "Run!" we marched; if he said, "March!" then we ran. "Run up the wall" meant "sit on the floor," etc. It kept one thinking all the time, and if you got it wrong, then you were on a charge.

Daily, just for exercise, we would do a thirty-mile yomp in full kit and carrying a rifle. On the return one day, we were just entering the barracks gate, and we were told to smarten ourselves up and march into the place as if we were sailors. (What were we then, if not?) By this time, we were just descending the hill approaching the barracks gate, and I heard a voice say, "Christ, my feet are covered in blisters."

The instructor shouted, "Prove who spoke!" No one answered. "Right, then, arms at the port!" Then we had to raise our rifles over our heads and double up and down the hill after having just run thirty miles.

The bloke next to me whispered, "Christ, if I had a bullet for this rifle, I'd shoot that bastard."

But that didn't help; he just kept us running up and down the hill till late at night. Several men dropped from exhaustion.

For our training, we had to take command of large parties of men and shout out instructions to them whilst drilling them on the parade ground. More than one poor soul shouted out, "Forward march!" and then, when the men were halfway across the parade ground, "Halt!" but unfortunately for them, the front half never heard, so they just kept marching, and they would have to run after them and bring them to a halt. They never passed the course.

We had to get them to form square and do many other manoeuvres on the parade ground, and it was strange to see what a mess they could finish up in if one was not careful. Anyway, I passed this course successfully, so now I was a fully established leading wireman, and I could now wear badges of crossed torpedoes on my right arm, my hook on my left, and my combined ops badge on my left wrist. We were all very proud of the combined ops badge: it was a hook (or anchor) together with an airplane prop and a tommy gun.

I got another draft chitty, and I was off to Scotland, where we learnt about camouflage. The Japanese were nap hands at this. We were given examples: one would enter an empty field (or so one thought), and one couldn't see a soul. Then, wonder of wonders, all the trees and bushes started to move, and men came out of hollows in the ground with branches on their hats and so on, and there were about one hundred facing you.

One lad was a bit fed up with the whole affair, so he made a bunk for it. He was finally cornered at the railway station, so he threw himself under a train, and he came out of the episode without any legs. We had to guard him in hospital twenty-four hours a day in case he did himself any further damage.

At the end of the course, we were given a rare night off ashore, so we all got thoroughly Brahms and Liszt. Coming back along a country road in the dark, I was given a dare to jump over a ten-foot wall. Naturally I did it, but I hadn't been told that there was a twenty-foot drop on the other side onto rocks. But as I was relaxed, I didn't hurt myself, and all the lads thought it was a good joke.

One of our party thought he was the bee's knees for bravery, so he said, "I'll show you how to tackle this assault course." He grabbed hold of one of the ropes tied to a tree and swung out over the valley, and then, to our amazement, he let go. We rushed down to him, but it wasn't any good: he had broken several bones in his body, so we had to wait with him till the doctor and tiffies arrived.

The Cruise

Here we were, anchored on the trot in Poole Harbour early in 1944, and I had been promoted to leading seaman, hooky, killick, or whatever anyone cared to call me. Who would want to be in charge of such a motley crew, though, where threats of punishment meant nothing, as these lads took no instructions from anyone and laughed in the face of death?

The order came to cast off. It was a lovely evening, and over by Brownsea Island, the Lysander flying boats were anchored all in a line. The trot was full up with landing craft of all types – landing craft tank, landing craft rocket, and many other types – so something big was about to happen soon. The fishing vessel chugged its way along the inner harbour to the boom; we could use our engines until we cleared our own minefields, and then we had to use our rigging. The trot boat was picking up matelots and royal marine commandos from the landing craft and taking them ashore at Poole jetty for a night's spot of leave and the pubs (lucky blighters). We made our way into the outer harbour, and there all the motor torpedo boats were really buzzing, all being loaded with fuel and ammunition and warming up their engines. They were obviously on some action or other tonight, and some of them wouldn't be coming back (poor bastards), whereas we were just going for a cruise along the channel.

Dusk was falling as we made our way out past our own minefields and headed for mid-channel. Then the skipper called for me. "Hooky," he said pleasantly, "how does Hoppy always manage to fetch me a full cup of kye, no matter what the weather is like and no matter how the craft pitches and turns?" I didn't like to tell him that before Hoppy left the galley, he always took a mouthful of the skipper's kye out of his cup and then put it back in the cup before entering the skipper's cabin.

His cabin was full up with charts and bits of paper of all kinds, whereby he was able to chart our way through the British minefields; he also had all the latest information about the new German minefields. "Tonight," said Skip, "we are going inshore to the French mainland to pick up some very important personnel that have to be brought out no matter what."

Gee, thanks, I thought.

"So you will pick four men to take two dinghies ashore and pick them up. The MTBs are going to cause a diversion farther up the coast so that we can pull in without any problems."

We had cut our engines some way back and were now proceeding as if we were doing a night's fishing with the nets placed along the decks, but all of us were keeping watch to see if there were any loose mines or any E-boats in the vicinity. We could now see the French shore, and we were sailing along the coast, looking for a signal. Yes, there it was, about two miles farther along.

As we made our way along the shore, I tapped Hoppy, Lofty, Brommy, and Scouse on the shoulder, and they all nodded in silent acknowledgement and made to get the dinghies ready. (Christ, these nutters took notice of silent orders better than they obeyed verbal ones, so in future I would know how to dish them out.) We dropped anchor just offshore, and the lads began busying themselves as if they were going to do a night's fishing. Then the five of us lowered the two dinghies over the side, got down into them, and rowed for the shore.

The moon was just breaking through the clouds as we pulled the dinghies up onto the beach. We lay on the beach, observing, and to my consternation, I could see two sentries up on top of the cliff, and under the cliff lay about eight blokes, four of them armed to the teeth. I looked at Hoppy and Lofty and then nodded toward the sentries. In the dull light, I could see Hoppy's face break into a grin; here was one hard-hearted campaigner. Lofty just had a glazed look on his face. I looked at Brom and Scouse and nodded towards the eight guys huddled under the cliff, and they both slid along on their bellies in the direction I had indicated. Good, this – a piece of cake. Just nod and it was all done for you.

Later the two sentries just disappeared, so I thought it safe to stand up to see where the lads were. Suddenly, it was as if I had been hit by a train in the middle of my back; I had stars going round in my skull and in front of my eyes. I dropped to the ground and pretended I was dead, and as I was lying on my back, I managed to half open one eye to see a ten-foot Kraut guard standing over me with his rifle pointed at my stomach. He eased his rifle away and leaned over to search my clothing, to see if I had any arms in my possession. That was his mistake. My hand slid down to my knife in my sea boot, and I gently eased it out. Then I made one almighty thrust up under the ribs and into his heart, as I had been taught. I pulled his helmet back to throttle him, but he was already dead.

I was shaking, I had stars before my eyes, and I didn't like doing it at all. But it was him or me, and these were the bastards that had made my sister a widow. (Poor Maurice hadn't wanted to kill anyone, so he joined the RAMC so that he could tend to the wounded. He was stationed in Dover Castle – later that area of England was known as "Hellfire Corner" – and he was killed in 1942 by German long-range shelling.)

Hoppy and Lofty came back grinning, and the others all made haste back to the dinghies. We seated the VIPs in the dinghies, and then, with a wave to the French escorts, we started to row for the fishing vessel.

Nothing much happened on the return journey, but there was one hell of a fight taking place farther up along the coast where the MTBs were operating. When we had cleared the German minefields, for some unknown reason our MTBs gave us an escort, although we had never had this before, as we were loners. We started our engines and proceeded with what we thought was undue haste across the channel, but the MTBs were buzzing round us like wasps, trying to make us go faster. We arrived back in Poole and anchored on the trot, thinking we had earned our hard layers this last couple of days.

Later a trot boat came out with more gold braid on it than I had ever seen in my life – I think all the admiralty was present, and they welcomed our passengers. After things had quieted down, I took my aching head and back along to give them a good wash and a change of pants. Hoppy and Lofty were sitting in our mess, sharpening and cleaning their knives, and Brom and Scouse were playing fists. I just felt like being sick.

Later, when we sitting in our mess, I asked the lads, "Where's Lofty?" No one knew, so I went aloft to find out. It must have been a full moon that night because Lofty was prowling around the deck with an axe in his hand. "What are you doing, Lofty?" I asked. Just then, the midshipman came out of his quarters, and Lofty let out a horrible yell, raised the axe in the air, and ran after the midshipman. I shouted out for help, and with two of the other lads, we tackled Lofty and we all sat on him; then we had to get him down below and make him stay there. We never saw the midshipman for the rest of that night, but it must have been good training for the lad to know that he was being well looked after by combined ops personnel.

Buzz Bomb

It was May 1944, and I was with a flotilla of assault landing craft on Haying Island. All leave had been cancelled, but no one knew why. My mate George and I decided that we would go up to the Smoke to see my old man, as Mum, Dolly, and Carol were staying at Smethwick near Birmingham to get away from the air raids for a while. We jumped on a train to London, and when we got to Clapham Junction, all the servicemen opened the doors of the carriages and flung themselves out. (The train didn't stop there, but if we carried on to Waterloo, we were bound to be picked up by the military police.) As the train was travelling at about thirty miles per hour, about thirty servicemen were rolling along the station in a cloud of dust, and as none of us had tickets, we were able to walk out of the station unchallenged, as no one was expecting anyone to get off the train.

The following morning, George and I had quite a few bevvies and "decided to go and see Dolly's in-laws." The old man followed at a discreet distance to keep an eye on us. On our way round to see friends, we were in Wandsworth Bridge Road when an ear-splitting noise rent the air, and there above us was a torpedo with wings. Neither of us had seen a doodlebug before, and we went into the road to get a better view.

I shouted to George, "Its engine has cut out!"

The old man rushed up to us and shouted, "Take cover! It's a buzz bomb!"

We were too excited to take cover, and the silence was deafening. The bomb came down on an area a couple of streets away, on the corner of Bagley's Lane and Harwood Terrace, where I was born. We continued our journey, only to find that the bomb had dropped on and devastated a large area, including the house that we were going to visit.

Iris's father, George, was lucky: he had been lying on his bed upstairs, and when he heard the flying bomb, he ran downstairs and got under the staircase. (It's amazing that with all the devastation, the staircase always remains intact.) Anyway, he was unscathed apart from shock. Poor Iris, his daughter, had copped a load of glass in her scalp and had to have all her hair cut off. I went to see her in hospital that evening, and she was so embarrassed, but as she used to write to me, I had to make sure she was okay.

They were the lucky ones. There were many others that weren't so lucky. Afterwards, George and I were covered in muck and dust, so Aunt Doll and her neighbours sat us both on chairs in the street with a cup of tea. They then brought out their galvanised baths and scrubbing boards, took all our clothes off of us, and stood there in the street, washing the clothes (even though their windows and doors had been blown in and parts of the ceilings collapsed), as we had to get back that night. That was the wartime spirit.

One expects to see servicemen die in a war, but the indiscriminate killing of civilians is inexcusable.

The Sergeant Major

We'd been over to Rosyth and were coming back along the Firth of Forth, wearing our working khakis and with our faces covered with burnt cork; I'll bet we looked a mess. I had cut my conk open, and it didn't half hurt. We got as far as South Queensferry, and anchored out in mid-stream were several warships, destroyers, and aircraft carriers. Suddenly the engine in our landing craft decided to blow up, and all we could do was drift. We passed alongside a battlewagon standing there in all its glory, polished as if to shine in the dark, and there on the foredeck stood the officer of the day, all polished and gleaming.

We shouted up at him (two miles above our heads), "Oi, Charlie! Send us down a bucket of water!"

He looked over the rails, his nose turning up, and in his best Cambridge accent shouted, "Get that bloody heap away from my ship!"

Gee, thanks; nothing like knowing who one's friends are. Anyway, we filled up our radiator (I'll not tell you how) and pulled over to our combined ops base in South Queensferry. After we landed, the sick bay tiffy said that he couldn't repair my nose, as I would have to have it stitched, and I would have to go to Edinburgh Castle and see the doc. He kindly gave me a towel to put over my nose, and then I had to catch a bus into Edinburgh, as there were no ambulances available, and anyway, I was walking wounded.

I was sitting in the RAMC majors' waiting room, talking to the sick bay tiffy, when all of a sudden, in walked a squaddy, and the whole room lit up with his presence. It was a sergeant major, and with his stick under his arm, he rapidly walked up and down the room, looking well groomed, polished, and fit as a fiddle. He was called straight into the doc's surgery. Obviously I was not very important, as I was only bleeding a bit, and anyway I had my blood-red towel.

I said to the tiffy, "Doesn't look as if there's much wrong with him."

"Oh," said the tiffy, "he's got syph."

"Can you cure him, then?"

"No," said the tiffy. "If we gave him too many drugs, we'd kill him, so all we can do is keep it in check."

"What a personality he's got, though," said I. "The whole room lights up in his presence."

"Yes," said the tiffy, "the syph does that."

So now if anyone comes into a room and lights it up with his personality, I console myself by thinking, *Oh, poor bloke, he's got syph.*

Wartime Inventions

I went by train to Kings Cross and then had to catch another train to Lowestoft. The journey took about eleven hours, and all the way we were stopping because of air raids. I reported to the office of the master at arms on arrival and was given accommodation on the first night in the London co-op canning factory. I was told not to use the showers, as there had been an outbreak of skin infection. Several of the matelots that had caught it looked as if they were covered in woad: they had to put a blue unction on the affected places.

The following morning, I reported to the landing craft tank flotilla that I had been assigned to, and the skipper told me in no uncertain terms what he expected of me. I learned a lot from the wiremen and others that were working with me, and the following descriptions are of the inventions.

On the stern of the LCT, there was a metal tripod, and the boffins had invented this. When one beached on the enemy beaches, if one was dive-bombed by low-flying aircraft, then one fired a rocket from this tripod, and in the air a parachute would open up, and the charge would blow the aircraft out of the sky. Unfortunately, if the settings on the explosive charge were not set correctly, then it would drop back onto the craft that had fired it and blow that out of the water. So this device was not used very much.

Now, the crafty Germans had invented a magnetic mine. Let me explain. All boats had an inherent polarity, depending on whether they were north or south of the equator. The magnetic mine was attracted to this magnetism and then blew the ship out of the water. The boffins had invented the M coil to neutralise the polarity of the ships. This consisted of thirty turns of cable wound round the entire ship's hull. When charged, this neutralised the magnetism of the ship. I checked the polarity of the M coil on one craft, and then asked to see the skipper.

Very abruptly, the skipper said, "Yes, Hooky, what do you want?"

"Skipper," I said, "has this craft been south of the equator?"

The answer was in the affirmative. "Why?" he said.

"Well," said I in my best tone, "all the time you've been sailing on her, it's been *attracting magnetic mines.*

The M coil has never been reversed when crossing the equator."

The skipper turned a bit pale and said, "You had better put it right, then."

Well, I never asked for a medal, but I thought he might have said thanks or something.

I found out later why there were so many vacancies for wiremen on board the smaller craft. When in action, one of my jobs was to be right up forward and to wind the ramp down as we approached the beach, to let the tanks and marines run up the beaches so we could follow in with them. I did a few manoeuvres in the Scottish estuary called the Firth of Forth on landing techniques, and then we set sail again this time for my beloved Poole Harbour. Unusually, we tied up alongside the pier in Poole, so we were able to get ashore quite frequently. Now, on the back of the LCT, there was a kedge (or a very large anchor, Grandson). The object of this was that just before beaching on a raid, one would drop the kedge into deeper water and then beach. If one had to get off the beaches and the tide had gone out, then, by the use of the capstan, one could pull on the chain and the kedge and pull the craft into deeper water.

At the end of the jetty, the trot boats (manned by seagoing Wrens) were coming and going all the time, out to the craft moored on the trot. One particularly dirty night, the rain was pouring down, and there was quite a swell on the Ogin. It was the usual custom for all the marine commandos to take the P out of the seagoing Wrens and the officers, which were given covered seating in the stern of the trot boat. The trot boat was full to the brim with combined ops personnel returning from leave with their kit bags and rifles. The poor Wren got really flustered, and instead of putting the trot boat into forward gear, she put it in reverse. The trot boat reversed at very high speed straight onto our kedge, which didn't do it much good, as it knocked a hole in the bottom of the trot boat.

The boat sank, and all the personnel on board were ejected into the water. Now, it's a crime for a marine commando to lose his rifle, so in the water they held them above their heads, but with full kit on, it took some doing to grab their rifles and pull them out of the Ogin. I've never seen so many marines bobbing about in the ocean. Laugh? I nearly drank my own beer! But most of them took it good-naturedly, although many lost their possessions.

During this time I was transferred to a base mobile unit where repairs of all types were carried out on various craft. A new craft had been invented, called a landing craft rocket (LCR). These looked like a load of scaffold poles standing in line on the upper deck. The rockets could be fired all at once or a quarter at a time. It was stated after trials that a LCR could do more damage in an hour than the biggest battlewagon firing all day; the only trouble was that they were non-directional. These craft were so secret that no one told the poor wireman that when checking the firing elements of the rockets, an admiralty-type megger *was not to be used*. As this megger could pass up to one third of an amp, when the wireman tested for continuity of the firing elements, he could fire the rockets and blow himself up at the same time.

Another invention was the landing craft guns, and these were used on the Walkeren Islands Attack. Two large guns were mounted on the foredeck and were fired by marines. The instructions issued were that before firing the guns, the bilges were to be filled so as to stabilise the craft. With the craft stabilised, the marines fired the forward guns, and the recoil pushed many of the craft below the water line, and they sank.

Some of the inventions were a bit crazy, but we were a long way from using towed coal barges with forward ramps cut in them that were manufactured in Chelsea basin. So now we were on the attack.

Don't Wave — We're British

Tanner was a cousin of mine; he was also a member of the Royal Navy beaching party. He came to me and asked me which lading craft was the best one. I told him that the LCT64 was the easiest to start, as with the others one had to put paraffin waste up their exhaust pipes to get them started.

He related the following story to me:

The American servicemen had loads of cash and could get anything from the PX, from chocolate to nylons. Their uniforms looked as if they were made in Saville Row, whereas ours were chucked at us, and we had to make them fit by using needle and cotton.

It became the norm for anyone to go up to an American serviceman and ask, "Got any gum, chum?"

They were welcomed everywhere. In France and Germany, they also had the pick of the girls, whilst in general we just looked on. When we in combined operations had to get landing craft infantry ready to cross the Rhine in case they were needed, the LCIs were loaded onto low loaders to travel through France and Germany, and some wag painted on the side, in big white letters, "Don't wave – we're British."

Court-Martial

I had repaired the jeep and was test-driving it round the very narrow paths of Hayling Island. As I was going round a hairpin bend, a woman in a sports car drove quickly round on the wrong side of the road, causing me to swerve. As she passed me, she shouted out, "Cow!"

I opened the window of my jeep and wished her a "sailor's farewell."

I put my foot on the accelerator, went round the bend, and promptly hit a cow up the posterior.

Back at the combined ops base (a holiday camp in peacetime), an oppo asked if I would change watches with him, as it was his birthday. This didn't mean me doing very much, just looking after the duty watch, and as I hadn't any intention of going ashore that night, I agreed. After tea, I was sitting in my hut reading when the loud hailers boomed out, "Stand by, duty watch. Duty Killick, report to the guardhouse."

That was me. I walked down and reported to the regulating officer, and he said, "Hooky, a rating has broken ashore. Round up the duty watch, and go out and fetch him back. He's quite harmless."

I assembled the watch of nine men, and out the gate we marched. We passed a load of squaddies, all with rifles over their shoulders, and various columns of Americans, all equipped with four-foot-long truncheons and sidearms, but we didn't even have a torch between us. But then, the guy we were looking for was harmless.

As it was pitch dark by now, and of course there were no lights anywhere in these narrow roads, we carried on our merry way, looking for this matelot. A runner came up to us and told me that there was a disturbance reported in the back garden of an isolated house. We marched to this house, which stood isolated in the gloom, and as nothing could be seen, it was up to me to jump over the wall to see what was causing the disturbance.

There on the lawn was a matelot, flat out, obviously Brahms and Liszt. I searched him and found a sharpened bayonet in his sea boot, which I promptly removed. I ordered the lads to pick him up and carry him by his arms and legs, and thus we proceeded along the lanes back to our base. As we got to the gate, he started to stir, and then he became violent. I told the lads to put him on the ground and sit on him.

The duty officer came over and said, "Enough of that! Pick him up and take him to the regulating office."

He said to me, "Are you having trouble with him, Hooky?"

To which I replied, "Yes, sir."

He said to the duty watch, "Hold him."

Then he gave the rating an almighty blow to the chin. The rating didn't go much on this; he wrenched himself free and then grabbed hold of the duty officer's throat. We had to tear him away from the duty officer and again sit on him on the ground. I don't know why, but we never saw the duty officer again that night.

By now we had quite a crowd round us watching, and someone brought out a plank of wood and some handcuffs from the regulating office. We laid the plank of wood on the rating's back and handcuffed his wrists behind the plank. He lashed out with his legs, kicking us, so we had to bind his ankles to the plank as well.

I said to him, "Don't be so silly. You are making it worse for yourself," and I lit up a cigarette and went to put it in his mouth.

He spit it out and proceeded to bite me. He looked at me with intense hatred in his eyes and said, "I've killed many people before, and I am going to kill you."

We carried him into an empty hut to try to get some sense of realisation into his nut, but there were crowds of ratings trying to look in through the door. All this time he was snapping like a dog with rabies, and white saliva was drooling from his mouth. About four hours later, the chogi van arrived from Portsmouth with a load of Royal Navy police, and with him still shouting out that he was going to return and kill us all, they took him away. The chalets that we were billeted in were very flimsy, so we put all the bunks up against the doors and windows so that if he escaped, he would have to awaken us before he could get in.

About a week later, I was carrying out checks on the flotilla of landing craft assault when the loud hailers summoned me to appear before the officer of the day. They had brought the rating over from Portsmouth under armed guard. A preliminary inquiry was in progress, before a commander, and various facts were laid before this court. It appeared that the prisoner worked in the petty officers' mess, and he would say to any of them that if they could get the bayonet off of him before he killed them, he would give them his tot for a week. He had also been found guilty of manslaughter in Italy, where he had killed two ladies. (So he wasn't harmless at all.) I was asked if the almighty thump the officer had landed had subdued the prisoner, to which I truthfully replied that it had made him worse. The officer then produced the sharpened bayonet (as if he had disarmed the man), and I was asked if it had been in the possession of the prisoner. At the conclusion, it was stated that this trial would go to a higher court.

Another week passed, and I was summoned again, this time in front of a captain, and again after hearing the evidence, it was adjourned for a higher court. The next time the court was assembled, it was in front of a rear admiral, and at its conclusion, the prisoner was sent to chogi for fifty-six days.

As they took him back to Portsmouth, he whispered in my ear, "I am still going to get you, Hooky."

That was sixty-four years ago, and I am still trembling in me boots.

Demobbed

It was difficult to settle down after the war; I was like a caged lion. I now had a wife and son, but there were no homes for heroes to live in, as most of London consisted of large piles of rubble where houses had once stood. But then I had never been a hero; I had just done what I was told. My wife, my baby, and I had one room in my mother-in-law's council-requisitioned flat in Boundary Road. (I think it was where Douglas Bader rented a room during his Hendon days.) As we had no recognised accommodation and coal was now rationed, we were not eligible. Therefore, much to my consternation, my wife and son spent most evenings during this cold winter with mother-in-law, in her front room. This didn't please me, so I went down to Kilburn for a drink in a pub. There I was, minding my own business, when a booming voice bellowed out, "Hello, Hooky."

It was Hoppy. He inquired how I was doing in Civvy Street, and I told him about the wife and son, also that I was doing very well earning over six pounds a week as an electrician. He in turn said he had his own business and thought I wasn't doing all that well, as by working nights, he was earning fifty pounds a night. As he was doing so well, he was now looking for a partner to expand his business – was I interested? Certainly I was, but what was his business? He told me he was doing shops and had all the equipment necessary. Well, I wasn't put out; I didn't mind doing hard graft like washing down and painting for fifty pounds a night.

"When are you doing the next one, Hoppy?" I asked.

"Tonight, after closing time. Can you start straight away? I need help badly."

At closing time, I followed him along the Kilburn High Street to the shop where he was going to work. He approached the shop door and took a jemmy out of his coat pocket, and then he turned to me and said, "Right, you stand there, and if you see any rozzers coming, let me know."

I went home to my wife and child.

Civvy Street

During the war, I was at several combined ops bases in Scotland, South Queensferry, Bo'ness, Aberdeen, and other places farther north. Everything was grey stone – the houses and loose brick walls separating the fields – and I thought, *Wouldn't it be nice to see some brick again?*

I got a draught chitty to deepest Cornwall, and I thought, *Hurrah,* but when I got down there, again it was all grey stone. To those that don't believe me, let me say that my first call was to Plymouth and Devonport, and there the whole area had been flattened, and it was a mountain of grey stone rubble (which has since been rebuilt, with red brick), and the only thing standing was a church spire.

After I was demobbed, I used to go round all the pubs in Wapping, and also to the Prospect of Whitby. I used to see some great turns in those pubs. In those days, I used to go to Greenwich Power Station from Hertfordshire. I'd given up smoking so that I could buy a tube for the TV I had made out of old aircraft radios. When one got to the docks, all the dockers used to pile into the nonsmoking compartments, puffing away at their ticklers. Someone told me I should have told them to put their fags out, but that would have been a foolish thing to do.

In 1947, after demobilisation, when my mother came over to our lodgings, it was the first time that she had seen a television set, and she kept popping round the back of the set. I asked her what was up, and she said, "I want to see the girl on the end of that chorus line." So she kept going round the back of the set to see her! In those days, it was the Tiller girls, and later on Ford named a car after them; it was called Allegro.

Fortunately, I had made my set very robust, and in 1953 for the coronation, all the commercial sets kept burning out, as they weren't man enough to stay on for seven or eight hours. So I turned out to be the only bloke in the street to have a TV for the coronation, and the woman next door arranged for everyone to come into my house to see the spectacle, without me or the ex-wife knowing. When I got home from working a night shift, I found my house full up with all the neighbours, and I had to go to bed to try to get some rest.

In the early days, I used to do loads of jobs for other people. I installed doorbells, mended TVs, and repaired watches and clocks, and the people always rewarded me with ten Players' worth – about one shilling (or five pence in today's money), and they would think that they had treated me well. The crunch came when I was asked to repair a very old eight-day clock, so off to Clerkenwell I went to try to get the parts. After many trips to different clock shops, I had to buy the complete hairspring movement, and it cost me thirty shillings (or one pound fifty pence in today's money). I made a good job of it, and the customer again rewarded me with ten Players. I decided then that I wasn't going to do any more work for other people but work on my own thing instead. So I put all my spare stamps into a club book and got my cash back. At least I was dealing in something that was my hobby; that is, foreign stamps.

Seven O'clock Club

I don't know whether they mess about with your tea now, but from the ages of seventeen to twenty-one, I had various amounts of bromide added to it, and after fifty-five years, it's just beginning to work.

I went to see a doctor, and he asked, "Do you smoke after sexual intercourse?"

I said, "I don't know. I've never looked."

It was about 1950; I had been demobbed for four years and now had a good job in London Transport sub-stations on shift work, and I was earning six pounds for a fifty-six-hour week. I was also going to night school four evenings each week, but if I was on shift, I had to change shifts with someone else. In my spare time, I was also cleaning windows, decorating, or emptying dustbins at a block of flats so that I could earn a bit more to take the family on holiday. (I forget when I had time to sleep.) So you can understand that I really looked forward to Friday nights, because after evening class, all my mates and I went for a few pints of beer in the West End. It was about eleven o'clock when I said good night to my oppos and made my way through Piccadilly Circus to catch my bus.

In Piccadilly there was a crowd gathering, and there in the middle was a very attractive young lady lying on the pavement. The normal comments were coming from the observers:

"She's drunk."

"Someone should do something."

Being a man of action, I thrust my way through the crowd and asked the distressed damsel if I could help.

She asked me to help her to her feet, and when I did, she stuck to me like a sink plunger. I asked if I could take her to her home, and she told me in which direction to go, but it wasn't home she wanted, as she had to meet someone at the Seven O'clock Club. When we arrived there, she was obviously known: when the grill was opened and they saw her with me, the bouncers opened the door and let us in. The place was a right dive; heavy smoke hung about, and the lights were so dim that it was difficult to see much, but all round the room there were curtained alcoves. I sat her at a table and went to the bar to get drinks. By now she was well and truly sober, and we sat chatting until she suddenly said she had to phone someone.

When she came back, she leaned over to me and said, "I am a plainclothes policewoman, and if I were you, I'd leave, because we will be raiding this club in five minutes." I hastily made my exit and went home.

When I had finished my shift on Saturday, I was at home, sitting at the table, waiting for my dinner, and the *Evening Standard* lay at my right-hand side. I opened the paper, and the front-page headlines shouted at me: SEVEN O'CLOCK CLUB RAIDED. Drugs had been found, and many people were put into jail cells.

My wife came in with my dinner and said, "Did you have a good time last night?"

"Oh, so-so," I replied.

It isn't always to one's advantage to be a man of action, especially when the opposite sex is involved, but still, we can't change what we are.

Ted

In those days, one worked hard, studied hard, and, when one found the time, played hard. Now, I had never had the urge to take every woman I met to bed; I suppose subconsciously I was not prepared to catch an unsociable disease and take it home to the wife, saying, "Look what I've got for you, darling!" I suppose I skirted round the edges a bit, just for the excitement; also, there were no birth-control pills in those days.

Well, here we were after evening classes at nine o'clock on a Friday night, after listening to the drone of the lecturer for three hours, so we decided on a pub crawl round the West End. At the back of the Palladium was a quiet pub where we always started the evening with a few bevvies. I opened the pub door and nearly fell into Martha Ray's mouth. She was a cute little thing, much smaller than one imagined from her films, but was her "north and south" big!

It took a couple of pints to get us back to normal. Sitting in one corner of the bar were a couple of ladies that said they were past debutantes – I think that they were past most things; apart from their smart appearance, they were well and truly three sheets to the wind. I couldn't understand their conversation either. Whilst eavesdropping, I heard one say to the other, "Oh, darling, how do you hold your liquor?"

The other replied, "Easy, sweetheart – I hold him by the ears."

Ted was the sales director of a large firm, and after a discussion, it was agreed that since he held all the membership cards for the West End clubs, we should visit a few. At the first club we visited, I was surprised to find a female friend that I used to know when I was a choirboy. She really had developed in the classical style. I was over six feet tall, but she looked down at me with fond remembrance in her eyes. She told me that we were going to have a dance, and I couldn't really object, as by this time she had me in a half nelson.

There wasn't much room on the four-foot-square dance floor. I couldn't do a syncopated whisk; with all the other dancers in close proximity, it was more like a smooch. There I was, my feet not touching the floor, pressed up against this Venus who had very little, if anything, on underneath, and I could feel every outline of her delicious body. The last time I had felt this pleasurable feeling in my groin was when I was in dancing classes when I was twelve. A young lady about my age rushed over to partner me when we were going to learn ballroom dancing. The instructor shoved us violently together, at the same time shouting out, "Hip contact!"

Wow, I liked that but didn't know what the feeling was whilst we were learning to dance. She obviously liked it as well. Every time the instructor shouted out, "Take your partners!" she ran over to me. But I didn't know that there was any difference between boy and girl.

As I was enjoying it and thinking of going to sleep in her arms, up came this seven-foot-tall guy built like a No. 2 double-decker bus, with a face to match.

He said to her, "Are you coming with me, or are you staying with him?"

She replied, "I am staying with my darling."

Now, I'm not one to boast – well, not much – so I said to her, "Who was that?"

She replied, "My husband."

The six of us made a rapid exit from the club, as none of us wished to meet him again in the dark, especially if he had gone home to get his sawed-off shotgun. We made a beeline for Piccadilly Circus. Now, it is said that if you stay in Piccadilly Circus long enough, you can be ripped off rotten by every crook in the world, or something like that, but then I never listen to idle gossip.

There we were, looking up at the lights, when this party built like Marilyn Monroe comes up, throws her arms round my neck, and gives me an almighty smacker. This did not surprise me, as it had happened many times before. I think I am singled out because I have a face like the back of a bus and some girls like to mother me, or maybe they don't believe that with a figure like mine, I can be alive and human at the same time, and they want to find out. It happened in Croydon with the nurses, in Oxford with the graduates, when I played with the Haymakers, on Chelsea embankment, and here in Folkestone. Maybe I will write about that some other time.

The difference this time was that she didn't let go or run away; she just hung on there like a black widow spider with me in her web. The other lads saw that I was temporally engaged and left me there all by myself (apart from her, of course). They didn't even try to lift her off, lousy lot. As she held my waist tight, I didn't have a chance to do the normal Irish whip and get away.

After two or three more smackers, she whispered in my ear that she was with the police and was pretending to be drunk. All she wanted was to get near a bloke that was sitting on a seat in the middle of the Circus. He was a dangerous criminal and had to be arrested, and I was going to be the dupe. Warning bells sounded in my ear like Big Ben; subsequently I realised that here was this party acting like an alcoholic in love with an empty bottle, but her breath had no smell of alcohol.

Anyway, with her laying her head on my shoulder and pretending to stagger, I crossed the busy road and took her to the middle of the Circus, where she staggered up to the bloke in question. Suddenly there appeared loads of coppers, and she arrested this bloke. Blimey, it was the seven-foot-tall guy that was married to the Venus! He saw me and lashed out, but I had already run away back to my home.

(Please note: if in future I am approached by a young, pretty, shapely female, I will ask to see her particulars first, before she hangs on my neck or kisses me.)

Living In Hertfordshire (Where 'Urricanes 'Ardly Ever 'Appen)

Having moved from my mother-in-law's requisitioned flat, I now lived in one room with my wife and two children. The room cost over half my salary. I had completed building my first television from old government surplus radios. After I had tuned the set in, I had a picture that was upside down. My door was open, and a Nigerian who occupied the next room spotted the TV. Now, he had never seen a TV picture before, and he came into our room and spent all night with his head upside down, looking at the picture. I was anxious to get rid of him, as I wanted to shut down the set and reverse the coils, and I needed to put the kids to bed, but he wouldn't go away.

Later we were lucky enough to get a terraced house on a new estate in Hertfordshire. Around 1954, I was working on night shift at a power station. I caught the morning bus home, and a neighbour was on the same bus. He sat next to me and started shouting about no one wanting to do an honest day's work anymore.

All the kids down the street, when asked what they wanted to be when they grew up, wanted to be like Mr. M, who was obviously a banker in the city, as he went off every morning in a smart suit, carrying a briefcase. One evening, I was walking through Soho and Leicester Square when I stopped to watch the buskers who were entertaining the crowds queuing for seats in the cinema. An old banger arrived; the blokes in the back changed into their Egyptian costumes, and out came the sand dancers. They were very entertaining, but I noticed with surprise that one of them was my neighbour Mr. M, the one the kids thought was a city banker.

One morning after finishing a night shift, before catching the bus at Burnt Oak, I walked along the shops. It was a regular trip for me to pick up a bag of broken biscuits at the baker's, as the kids loved them. I carefully put them in my briefcase and then proceeded to the bus stop, as the buses only ran every half an hour. One bus was just leaving, so I ran after it and jumped on the running board. I tripped, and in doing so, my briefcase opened, and all the biscuits fell out on the floor. The clippie looked at me with a grin on her face, saying, "I often wondered what you carried in those briefcases. Now I know."

Boy, was my face red.

As Borehamwood was a new town, the buses stopped running at seven o'clock in the evening, but my late turn at the power station didn't finish until 10.00 p.m. So at the termination of the buses, I then had a five-mile walk home every evening.

One evening while I was passing the bus stop, I saw a young lady waiting there, and I told her that all the buses were finished for the night and that she would have to walk home. She asked if I would escort her, as most of the walk was unlit through the country. I told her to tag along with me. But all the way home, she was talking about personal things: her husband worked on the railway; she had been to see her boyfriend, who lived in London, but he was very young and didn't know much about ladies. She then started talking about her clothes, and her bras cost quite a bit, but her knickers were very cheap. When we got near to where she lived, she asked me to come into her house after she had sent the babysitter home; I would have to be careful, though, because she fell very easily (there were no birth-control pills in those days). When we got to her house, she went in, and I said goodnight to her and went home to my wife and children. I had many offers like that one, but I always refused, as I never committed adultery.

I had four children in all: three older boys and Anne. I used to run three football teams to keep the lads up to scratch. I had the eleven-to-thirteens on Sunday mornings. They were playing a cup match one day away from home, and watching them next to me was a proud mother.

She said to me, "Isn't my son a good footballer? And he's only seventeen!"

He played for the home team and this was for eleven- to thirteen-year-olds.

The three boys all went abroad when they were older: the eldest to Portugal, the next boy to Gambia, and the youngest to Jersey because the pubs were open all day. The middle son had polio when he was ten months old, and the hospital was going to send him away to a home in Carshalton, but as we proved to be good parents, they allowed him to stay with us. One shouldn't have any favourites with the children, but he was indeed my favourite. Even though he was paralyzed down the left side, we allowed him to play football, and he got as far as playing for the county; later he rode a scooter, skates, and then a motorbike.

When he was young, my wife had to take him to hospital in London, and it just shows how nasty some people can be – they put his arm into a brace so that he had it level with his shoulder.

On the bus, a man remarked to his wife, "There you are – these youngsters don't know how to look after a child. That one has broken his arm, and the parents should be ashamed of themselves."

This reduced my wife to tears, and she was still crying when I got home that night.

One bank holiday, my in-laws came over to visit us. I took them to the Horses' Home of Rest.

My father-in-law loved horses, so I took his photograph standing alongside the stables. One horse obviously didn't like him standing there and bit him in the shoulder; good job he had his overcoat on, otherwise the skin would have been penetrated.

The Haymakers' Tour

In those days, I played cricket three times a week, and invariably one would be asked to make the number up for some other team that was unable to field a full eleven. The Haymakers were a touring side made up of gentlemen farmers, and they had booked up to tour for a week playing various university teams at Camford. My mate Bernie wasn't doing anything that week either, so we both thought it would be a nice change. Bernie was a useful opening bat and worked as a salesman for a large brewery, but he seemed to play more cricket than sell beer.

On the appointed day, we reached our hotel in the university town and were met by a reception committee and promptly invited to visit one of the universities. We were given all the courtesy possible by our hosts and were very impressed by what we were shown. We were also impressed by the number of cans of beer that were consistently put into our hands, so it was only right that we, in turn, invited them to our hotel at lunchtime to reciprocate.

The matches took place in the afternoons and early evenings, and as by this time everyone had worked up a tremendous thirst, we all adjourned to the undergraduates' pub for the rest of the night. Now, I don't know if my memory is failing, but I don't seem to recall any particular day's events. That week just seems to be a bit of a blur, so I will recall what I can remember.

We were in our hosts' favourite pub, and after a few bevvies, we were the best of friends and singing their age-old songs. I remember that one young man was most insistent that I swap ties with him; mine had a sheaf of hay with a pitchfork stuck in it, and his was a plain old blue tie that one could buy from Woolworth's for sixpence. Obviously I was not going to swap ties; that is, until our newfound friend Cuthbert explained that the owner of the tie was a boxing blue, and then I couldn't swap it fast enough.

Our hosts were studying law and were the future legal brains of Britain, and this you could tell by their behaviour. Two more undergraduates walked in, and as they were friends of our hosts, they asked them if they would like a drink, and their reply was in the affirmative. The new lads unselfishly bought four pints, promptly poured them over our hosts' heads, and the hosts gave the impression that they enjoyed them up to the last drop. Later, of course, they returned the favour when they bought the next round. Bernie and I looked at each other askance, but it would have been unsociable of us to go down on our knees to lick up the precious fluid from the floor; still, it was good for Bernie's trade. It was obvious to us that these lads were getting a first-class education in fairness to equip them for their future role in the legal profession, as throughout the evening the general rule seemed to be "one pint in the stomach, and one over the head." So much so that by late evening, the bar floor had about three inches of ale washing about all over it, and we were getting our socks wet.

For some reason, Bernie had to go outside, and as he had been gone for some little while, I went myself to ensure that he hadn't come to any harm. There I was, standing outside a lovely little pub in Camford on a beautiful summer evening when a little red sports car drew up at the kerb. A young lady swung her sheer-clad legs over the side of her car door, ran up to me, put her arms round my neck, and gave me an almighty smacker. (I do wish that sometime one of them would explain why they do this.) She ran back to her car and drove off. Bernie was just putting in an appearance as this happened, and the only conclusion that we could come to was that it had been a mirage.

When we got back into the bar, it was closing time, and the future brains of Britain were fully equipped with several large tins of party sevens, ready for a late night's studying. As there were only a few ladies in our company, they decided that on the way back, they would pick up some nurses that they knew would like to help us with our studies. Outside the nurses' home it was a bit late, so they decided that they would attract the nurses' attention by throwing stones at their bedroom windows. Now, I don't know if the stones they used were too heavy or if in their inebriated state they put too much pudding into their throwing. There was an almighty crash of glass, the window was thrown up, and an angry face with face cream and curlers appeared. Our hosts shouted, "Christ, the matron!" and bolted for their lives.

Naturally, Bernie and I followed with all haste, picking up the discarded party sevens as we fell over them. At the appointed meeting place, we all arranged ourselves comfortably on the settee (although I can never remember how twenty-two men and seven girls managed to sit on it) and during the course of the next few hours had a quiet but noisy drink, if you understand what I mean. Every time a party seven can was emptied, it was one legal beagle's party trick to allow the others to flatten the empty can on his head. First one side was crashed on his nut and then the other, until it was quite flat (the can, I mean). It was obviously part of his education that allowed him to do so, for if you have heard of the hanging judge, then this young man was in training to become a hard-headed judge.

When all the cans had been emptied and subsequently flattened, the legal brains were quite disappointed, but to show their resourcefulness, they took a large brass ornamental plaque off the wall and proceeded to flatten this on Hard Head's nut. By this time he was obviously very tired of the whole thing, for he sank to the floor and dozed off.

It was time for us to return to our hotel and for our hosts to return to their university quarters, but when we arrived at their university, all the gates were locked – and to listen to them, if they were caught, the penalty was worse than six months in Holloway. However, the age-old custom was put into practice by giving them a bunk up over a pair of large wooden gates. In our inebriated state, it was obvious that the person being lifted was being subjected to a hazardous situation. As an ignorant observer, I asked how long they had been going over the gate when there was a three-foot gap at the bottom that they could crawl under. I thought they were going to make me the attorney general.

Now, one of the peculiarities of our hotel was that there were probably about fifteen clocks in the vicinity that struck the hour. As they were all out of synchronism with each other, when midnight came, one had to count in unison with the chimes up to one hundred and eighty before one could relax and nod off. To lessen the number, I had removed the pendulum from the grandfather clock on our landing and surreptitiously slid it into Bernie's pillowcase.

Now, I have always found it strange that when retiring after a heavy drinking session, the liquid finds its own level in one's body and affects the eyesight; so to prevent this, I decided to inspect the hotel's plumbing and discard some of the offending alcohol. Unfortunately, the toilet was occupied, so I stood up against the wall, smoking a cigarette, with my eyes closed. I heard one o'clock chime, but as it was about three in the morning, it had to be Bernie crashing into his bed.

Just at that moment, there was a noise of the cistern flushing, and the door opened, and out dashed the mirage, who flung her arms around my neck and gave me another smacker. (I do wish they would explain why they do this.) Now, she had on the most flimsy of nightdresses, and after the embrace, I swear that I do not remember burning my pyjamas with a cigarette, but there was a large burn in the lower half of them. Just at this moment, Bernie came out of his room, rubbing the bump on the back of his head. "Where did she go, Bernie?" I asked.

He swore that she had jumped into her little red sports car and had sped off down the hotel corridor. I knew that wasn't true, as there was no sign of her exhaust fumes, so she must have gone up in a helicopter.

When we arrived home, my eldest son was waiting at the gate of our home.

"Did you win, Dad?" he cried.

Win? I don't even remember playing.

Cox's Orange Apple Tree

If I were a tank driver and I were liberating people, it would be just my luck for the crowd to cover my tank with flowers, as I suffer from hay fever. Then I would sneeze my head off and knock myself out when my head hit the roof. You always have to be careful when speaking English to a foreigner … or to your own children, come to that.

In Hertfordshire (where 'urricanes 'ardly ever 'appen), I took great care in growing a "Cox's orange apple tree," and to my great delight, I finally had two small apples growing on it. I told the children that under no circumstances were they to pick the apples.

They didn't, but one morning I went out to my beloved tree to find only two apple cores hanging from the branches. As they said, they hadn't picked them, but I hadn't said they couldn't eat them.

Sorry about that, but as with English, so with deeds. I always try to see the alternative to what other people are saying. Don't always go along with the crowd, and sometimes, if you feel you are right, do something different from what all the others are doing.

Fishing

One of the reasons for moving down to the South Coast was that I was a keen fisherman. Denge Marsh is one of the best places in Britain for sea fishing. So off I went when a mackerel school was inshore, and I was pulling them in five at a time every time I cast my line out. I came away with two dustbin bags full, far too much for my own needs, so I went round to all my neighbours and asked if they wanted any fish, and they all did. I took them all a carrier bag full up with them, but all the women screamed that they still had their heads on and the eyes were looking at them. So I had to fetch the fish home and top and tail them; you should have seen my kitchen after that lot. I haven't been fishing since.

Many years ago, I was course fishing in Hodderston, Hertfordshire. It was a lovely, sunny day, and all the regular fishermen were there, but nothing was biting at all. Come evening, a man and his wife took up a position next to me on the bank, and he prepared a line, handed it to his wife, and said, "There you are. You wanted to fish

– now cast in over there into the middle of the river." She dropped the line adjacent to the bank, and he screamed out, *"Not there, you silly cow! Into the middle of the river!"* Her float immediately submerged, and she pulled out the biggest tench you ever did see. All of us watching packed up our gear and went home empty-handed.

The Operation

I was now in my late thirties, and I had suffered pain for quite a while but just laughed at it. John was my local GP and a very good friend of mine. He called at my house one summer evening, and whilst I was talking to him, I had a very sharp pain that caused me to sink to the floor. He asked me what the matter was, and I answered (so as to be polite) that I had a pain up my sit-upon. He said, "If it's that bad, you had better come to my surgery, and I'll see what the trouble is."

The following morning, he examined me and told me that I had a fissure and that if it didn't get any better, then I would have to go to hospital. The trouble with any pain in the anus is that as the pain gets worse, the anus closes up. I went back to see him and told him that I was feeling better but I couldn't go to toilet, so he gave me a laxative. The pain got worse; I don't think anyone thought about painkillers in those days. Not only was there pain in my anus, but as I hadn't been to toilet, I was also having trouble and pain with wind in my stomach.

The only way I could get rid of the wind was to lie on my back in the front room, with my knees drawn up to my chest and my back made into a ball, and rock backwards and forwards. My wife and children thought that this was hilarious and would lie on the floor with me, and with them laughing their heads off, we would all rock backwards and forwards together until I managed to squeeze the wind out of my sit-upon.

I didn't get better, and the pain was so intense that I would run up and down the stairs, trying to leave my bum behind. The hospital was in City Road London and was for cancer of the bowel and bladder, which cheered me up no end. I made out a will and made arrangements with the bank manager so that my wife could have access to all the funds she required. So off to the hospital I went to see a surgeon, and my appointment was for nine o'clock in the morning. The waiting room was full, with two to three hundred people all waiting to get attention. Then, in the middle of an examination, the surgeon was called away to attend a critical case in the main wards. We were lucky if we got away before six o'clock at night. After examining me, it was found that I had trouble further up in the form of polyps, which would require an operation to remove. (My mother had just died from cancer of the bowel, and they had told her that she had polyps, so it didn't make me very happy.) I was told that I was to have three separate operations and that I might be in hospital for some time.

When I reported to hospital, I had a number of routine tests, including a chest X-ray. On the night before the op, I was given numerous doses of laxative, and then in the morning I was told that my op had been cancelled and I was to go home for the weekend. No one knew why, so I was left with the feeling that I now had lung cancer as well. Believe me, I was not happy that weekend.

I reported back to the hospital on Monday morning, and they told me that the reason the op had been cancelled was that they had made some new tools, including a miniature camera, and they could now do all the ops from the inside instead of cutting my skin on the surface. I had the op, and although it was painful afterwards, I enjoyed my stay in hospital. As there was an acute shortage of nurses, we all took care of one another, especially when a person was coming round from anaesthetic. It was as though we had all been transferred back to wartime, where we all sang songs, looked after each other, and, as we were all in the same boat, understood what the other fellow was going through. We had many a laugh despite the pain, and I made a number of friends whilst I was there.

One close friend was a high court judge, and he told me that he made an example of the youngsters that came before him. I pointed out that they were not all bad, as I had a number of lads that had been in trouble in the three football teams that I ran. One, for a lark, had pocketed a snooker ball on a dare, and he had been caught and sent to an approved school, but at heart he was a lovely lad. My friend was impressed and promised that before sentencing them in future, he would give due consideration to the points I had raised.

It was a laugh a minute; the surgeon examined my posterior and said, "Oh, damn, I've left tags."

I replied that it was okay, as the previous ones had fallen off. I didn't know what the heck he was talking about, but he seemed to be delighted with my reply. My mate Fred in the next bed hadn't been to toilet for over ten days. Every morning, the matron would come round and ask, "Have you been?"

Poor Fred replied, "*No.*"

"Right," the matron said, "you will have to have a suppository."

The following morning, there was the same question from the matron and the same answer from Fred. "Right," she said, "you'll have to have another suppository."

"Oh, not another one!" said Fred. "I can't swallow them."

To which I rejoined, "For all the good it did him, he might as well have pushed them up his jumper."

I was surprised by some of my visitors. My friend John took time off from his busy surgery to come and see me. He bought me a book called *Dr. No,* and I became a

James Bond fan. The chief engineer from work came in to see me, but my wife couldn't make it every day, as her duties in St. John's Ambulance Brigade kept her away.

When I was released from hospital, my friend drove me home, and I was overjoyed. I don't think my wife was very happy to see me, so I went down to the end of my garden and sat there in the rain, thinking about how happy I had been with all my mates in hospital.

A few weeks later, I had a letter. It was from the judge's wife. He had died, and she had found my address in his pocket.

Cindy

When I went to an auction and would be away for the day, I would give my wife a sum of money to buy herself something she wanted. When I returned, she would have bought the most cuddly beagle puppy I had ever seen … then another auction, another puppy, and so continue ad infinitum.

I firmly believe now that when the children grow up and leave home, a lot of women have to have a child substitute – be it a cat, a dog, a husband (if he is lucky), or a lover – on whom to bestow their love and affection. I didn't mind, as at least it kept her busy and close to me. Being very intelligent, she read all the books she could lay her hands on, listened to the hallowed authoritarians of the dog world, and spent two evenings a week and many hours of the day training her dogs. Naturally, in time, she went to more and more dog shows and began to have success in the ring.

I was very proud of her; I loved to see her win first the small shows and then championship shows. Soon she required a bigger house with more ground so that she could kennel her dogs more conveniently. She began judging, and I was so proud of her knowledge, competence, authority, and organisational expertise. I realised that as she was away from home more and more, in order to stay compatible, I also should purchase a puppy to show, and forego my own hobbies.

Eight weeks was a long time to wait from the time I ordered the puppy, and then I travelled hundreds of miles to go and see the litter when it was born. Ten balls of fluff were cuddled up to their mother; I didn't know which one to choose. Finally one wiggly-waggly tail waddled away from its mum and tried to eat my shoe. That was the one! Then I had a further wait of seven weeks before the puppy could leave its mother and I could bring it home. We called the puppy Cindy.

Thinking of the size of a fully grown Labrador, how was it possible for that ball of fluff to crawl under a low sofa and refuse to come out? At first she wouldn't eat, and I had to feed her with food on my finger. The lady breeder said that I was spoiling her.

She began to grow very rapidly. I remember the first time she saw snow: she was almost buried in it, wagging her tail and trying to eat the snow. In the summer, when the French windows were open, she would race down the garden when I came home from work. That winter, when the French windows were shut, she ran out through one pane of glass, gave me a wonderful welcome, and then ran ahead of me through another pane of glass, miraculously not suffering a scratch.

We went to a few shows and did well, and then – wonder of wonders – she got second at a championship show and was eligible for Crufts. My wife also had three dogs at the show. I didn't expect to win anything, as the Labrador classes were so large, but we gave it a try. Cindy behaved perfectly as we stood in front of the judge. I had titbits in my pocket so as to tempt her to stand correctly and be gone over, as it were, but I dropped all the titbits on the floor. Cindy thought I was giving her a treat and scrambled all over the ring to get her reward. The judge whispered in my ear, "Never mind, old man, it happens to us all."

Cindy was almost four years old when my wife suggested that she should have a litter before she became too old. I think I suffered as much as she did whilst she gave birth to nine glorious puppies. I never cease to wonder that without being told, taught, or otherwise informed, an animal knows how to bear and take care of her litter. She kept picking up one puppy and casting it aside with a whimper; I told her not to be silly and put the pup back on her nipple for it to feed. This happened several times. The pup died, and I know that Cindy was casting aside a pup that was not destined to live. I kept one pup for my daughter, and we named her Bumble; she was kept in a kennel with smaller dogs, and I'm certain this is the reason she became highly strung in later life.

When my wife left home, I went to the doctor's and told him I thought I was having a breakdown. He told me that I didn't know what pressure was and I should try being a doctor. (He was about twenty-five years old.) When I told him that my wife had left me after many years of marriage, he asked me if I was suicidal; I told him that if I was, I wouldn't kill myself with his drugs but instead drive my car into a brick wall. He insisted that I take the drugs prescribed and told me they were not habit-forming. (How wrong he was!) I threw them into the dustbin and told Cindy my tales of woe. She listened patiently then looked at me with her great big hazel eyes. She knew when I was sad and laughed when we were happy; she stood remote when required; she supplied affection, loyalty, and trust; and she even stood on her hind legs and danced with me when the occasion demanded. All she asked for in return was one meal a day, but who would look after her if I didn't have the will to carry on?

Five years passed, and I had to sell my house. My daughter moved into lodgings, and I moved away, taking Cindy and Bumble with me. A few girlfriends came and went, but in the main, we were alone. Bumble was a dog, but Cindy had human qualities: those great hazel eyes had all the understanding and trust that one could wish for, and her loyalty was always forthcoming. Maybe men also have a desire for a child substitute or grandchild substitute when one has never seen one's grandchildren.

When Cindy was fourteen years old, she began breathing heavily, and I could only walk with her for short distances before she sat down and looked at me as if to say, "Wait for me to get my breath back, Dad." She loved walking along the beach, where she walked in all the puddles with a mischievous look in her eyes. Bumble didn't like the water.

Later she began having trouble with her legs; her front leg would give way, and she would stumble. I tried to keep her as fit as I could by giving her short walks, but the day came when I took her across to the beach and she lay down and refused to go any further. I saw in her eyes that she was hurting, and after a long rest, she managed to walk home.

The lady vet said that I should have her put down. I was very sad. I tried to keep her going, but the pain in those large hazel eyes caused me a lot of heart searching. In the waiting room, she put her head on my lap, and I cannot describe what happened. I broke down. Here I was, a tough lad as a youth, volunteering for hazardous duties during the war, and now I was a soft-hearted old man.

Cindy's grave is at the bottom of my garden, and if there is a god on high and he allows humans to enter the animal heaven, maybe someday Cindy and I will meet again.

Sammy

Whenever I walked into the local pub, Sammy was there. It was obvious that he considered himself exceptionally popular and the life and soul of the party. He would constantly make asides about the people who came into the bar for a quiet drink, sometimes ignoring the protests that were made to him by the other regulars. He would think nothing of denigrating the others that drank at his table when they were not there. He clouded his activities of his so-called long service in the Royal Navy with hints and well-worn sayings of Navy slang. He had the largest cauliflower ear I have ever seen. By his remarks on the number of professional fights that he had fought, he received many free pints from the people who came to this holiday resort. To me he was a bit of a bore, and whilst I always called him by his Christian name, he referred to me as "son." Now, to him I may have looked young, and my service only consisted of three years in the Royal Navy during wartime, and even then I was glad to get out.

I was looking forward to Chris coming to stay for a week because there were many lonely people about, and I was one of them. Chris and I had known each other for some thirty years. Whilst I hadn't seen him for five years, I knew that our friendship would carry on from where it had left off: not having to force conversation, but instead quite content to sit in each other's company. He was a rough, tough Liverpool lad whose parents had brought him over from Northern Ireland when he was a boy. He had spent his youth in the Mercantile Marine, and later we both became qualified engineers in the power industry.

I knew that Chris had fought quite a few professional fights in his young, up-and-coming days and had been quite good. I had fought only a few amateur fights, and as a heavyweight, if I was onto a hiding to nothing, I became the fastest runner in the square ring. I was a bit dubious about taking Chris to my local; however, it was only round the corner, and we could have quite a few pints together and talk over old times.

As soon as we walked in, Sammy bellowed out, "Hello, boy!"

"Morning, Sammy," I replied.

Chris and I bought our pints and then sat at a table in the corner; meanwhile, Sammy seemed to have disappeared. "I see you've got Sammy down here, then," said Chris.

"Yes," I said, "do you know him?"

Chris related a tale from long ago. Sammy used to hang about the training gyms and would have been very pleased to get a bout. One evening, when Chris was fighting a contest ("middle billing," as it were), a preliminary fight would have had to be postponed, as one of the contestants was sick. But Sammy volunteered to stand in. It was his first and only fight. The bell rang for the first round, and Sammy came out from his corner and walked into an almighty windmill blow that landed on his right ear, and he went down for the count.

"What about his sea time?" I asked.

"Well, we did hear a bit about it," said Chris, "and as I understand it, he was in for two years long after the war, but he had never gone to sea, and then his parents bought him out."

Poor old Sammy. He was probably lonelier than I was, and whilst a lot of us magnify the truth somewhat and are a bit prone to exaggeration, he was trying to make up for it by proving to himself how popular he was.

When Chris had gone home to the Smoke, I again went round to my local.

"Morning, Sammy," said I.

"Morning, boy," said Sammy.

I smiled to myself. It was a lot easier to listen to him now, and at times, some of the things he said even caused me to chuckle.

The Tip

When he was sixty-five years of age, my old man retired from the gasworks as a fitter, and after thirty years' service he received seven and sixpence a week in pension. To help out his income, he got a job in a museum canteen washing up. After a couple of years, he slipped on a wet floor and was taken to hospital with a broken femur. He spent quite a while in hospital, so when he came out, I had Mum and Dad over to my place.

My old man was very keen on horse racing, and he would often have sixpence each way on his favourite horse (although betting at that time was illegal). At his local, all his mates would ask for his horse-racing tips. Anyway, to make a short story long, I decided to take him and Mum out to Newmarket because he had never been there. Mum, Dad, my wife, and my two children all jumped into my Chinese taxi cab (Cowley), and away we went.

As lunchtime approached, we stopped at a lovely little restaurant at Six Mile Bottom. We all had an excellent meal, and it cost two pounds ten shillings, so I left a half-crown tip on the table. In the car park, I had opened the car doors, and the old man came hobbling up to me on his stick, shouting, "Here, boy, take this!"

I told him not to be silly, as I could well afford to pay for the meal and I didn't want his contribution.

He was insistent that I take it, and he dropped a half crown in my hand, at the same time saying, "You haven't got money like that to leave on the table! Put it in your pocket."

He had decided that I shouldn't leave the waitress a tip and had picked it up from under my plate. Was my face red! With great haste I left the restaurant, and we hadn't travelled more than five miles down the road when my mum shouted, "Oh, dear, I've left my gloves on the table! Now we must go back."

Swimming

I have always been a strong swimmer. I suppose it's because when I was about four or five, my sister and I followed the Salvation Army band from our new house to the place where we used to live. Uncle Titch was standing outside with Aunt Doll, and he asked if I would like to go to Putney with him and his baby son. I was thrilled and said yes. He took us to the Thames at Putney, and whilst he sat on the shingle holding his newborn son, I was very happy pushing a stick along in the water. But I managed to fall into the water, and I remember seeing the fishes swimming as I went down. When I came up, I shouted out, "Uncle!" I went down again, and when I came up again, I shouted, "Titch!"

He put his newborn into the arms of some stranger and rushed over to where I was drowning. He said that he grabbed my hair and pulled me out, so I suppose I owe him my life.

Later in life, I got the twenty-five yard certificate at school when I was about ten. At a swimming gala I attended, a lady dived off the top board and swam underwater. I wanted to do that. I used to go swimming at the local baths quite a bit and soon learned to swim a couple of lengths underwater. I also loved diving and frequently would try out dives that my friends wouldn't try. I used to go home with a headache a lot, and I would go up to lie on my bed, but the old man would pull me up, saying, "If it gives you a headache, don't go swimming."

Later on, I used to go to the Greenford club, where I teamed up with another lad, and we used to do trick high dives. One of our favourites was Horse and Rider; I would sit on his back, and as he dived, I rode him down through the air. Another one was the inverted dive: facing me, he would bend over and put his head through my legs, and I would grab his ankles, and with him standing up and me upside down, he would dive off the high board. One day he suggested a new dive where he would put his head through my legs whilst I was facing away from him. He bent over, I faced away, and then he put his head through my legs, but before I could grab his ankles, he had dived. His hands operated as a fulcrum, and I was thrown though the air, coming down on the water with a lot of force, doing a very large belly flop. As there were lots of people watching us perform these high dives, they all got soaking wet, and when we came to the surface, all the onlookers were wiping themselves off with towels.

Rannoch Road Jam Factory was on the side of the Thames, and during the summer, Bill, who was a very strong swimmer, used to strip down to his trunks and go swimming from the wharf, and we all used to watch him. My mate, George said that I should go in the water as well, but no one told me about the strong current. I was about sixteen, but I was game, so I stripped down to my trunks and entered the water.

To my amazement, the current swept me away from the wharf, toward Hammersmith Bridge; I wasn't too worried, but I didn't like the look of the whirlpools around the bridge. I must have swum about three or four miles, the current all this time sweeping me farther and farther away from where I had entered the water. The only thing to do was to go with the current. I swam under the bridge and finally finished up about two miles away, on the other side of the Thames. I had to walk about five miles back in my bare feet, with only a swimming costume on.

Someone in a motorboat decided to carry out trials and just went up and down. I tried to shout for them to get out of the way, as I wanted to swim back, but either they couldn't hear me or they took no notice of the idiot on the bank. I walked way beyond the place that I was aiming for; finally the boat departed, and I was able to enter the water. I swam to the other side, but I was amazed: everyone had gone back to work. They must have given me up for dead.

Later, after I was demobbed, I used to go to the Hampstead swimming baths to practice my diving. One Sunday morning, I made a friend who also used the springboard quite a bit, he doing one-and-a-half-turn somersaults. All the girls used to run over to him and ask him if he was Anthony Newly, and he would reply yes.

I didn't have a clue who he was; I just carried on commenting about his dives. He also had his girlfriend there, who lived in Cricklewood. I later found out that he was the Artful Dodger in the film *Oliver*.

One day I did a Dead Man's Dive from the high board, into six feet of water, and split my head open. Holding a towel to my bleeding head, I got dressed and went to my doctor's. I didn't know it at the time, but he had committed suicide because of the atom bomb. I knocked and knocked at his door, but no one answered.

I went home to my wife, and she tried to get an answer from his surgery. We then tried several hospitals, but to no avail, as they all said that they didn't have an emergency department. All this time, my head was bleeding, and the only thing I had was my blood-red towel. It was about ten o'clock on Sunday morning, and then at about five o'clock, I finally got someone to see to my head at a hospital on the other side of the heath. They said that had I come earlier, they would have put stitches in it, but as it was now healing by itself, it was best to leave it alone.

I moved down to the South Coast because I have always loved the sea, and when the tide was on the turn, all the locals would sit on the stones, and some would go swimming. I used to love it, and I swam out farther and farther, until the folks on the stones were just dots. Then the incoming current took hold, and I was swept along much farther out than I imagined, but I kept on swimming; the only things I didn't like were jellyfish. Had it been the outgoing tide I would have been swept out into the channel. I swam much more than I intended: I was swept past Littlestone into Dymchurch. Now, Dymchurch was about eight miles from my home by road, but it was much shorter across the bay, so how far I swam, goodness knows. But after I landed, I had a problem. How would I get back to where I started with no cash, no towels, and no way to dry off? I got many strange looks whilst I was thumbing a lift, and I caused many a smile as well.

Lorna, Dear Lorna

I had been by myself for quite a while now, and I took myself off to Folkestone to do some shopping. As I passed Lea's Cliff Hall, I heard music, and as I had nothing else to do, I purchased a ticket to the tea dance. I sat at a table just to listen to the music, and to my surprise, several ladies came up and asked me to dance. The most attractive girl in the hall was sitting adjacent to the dance floor and always seemed to have a queue of men asking her to dance. To my utter amazement, she looked at me with a question in her eyes. I nodded, and she left all the other men standing and came over to me. She was heavenly to dance with, and we also jived together; she really knew her steps. At the end of the dance, I just went home, not thinking any more about it, as she was many years younger than I was. I didn't go back to a tea dance until about one year later. How was I to know that Lorna was saying to her sister and the other ladies at her table, "Wonder what happened to that man who smoked a lot? Perhaps he only came down here on holiday?"

In fact, I only lived twenty miles away.

I returned to the same location almost a year later and decided to go to the tea dance again. Whilst at the dance, some ladies asked me to dance, and Lorna came over to me to ask why I hadn't asked her to dance. I told her that I had no intention of getting on the end of her queue of admirers. We then arranged that when she looked in my direction, it would mean that she was asking me to dance, and we had most dances together. I really enjoyed dancing with her. She was excellent; no wonder all the men were at her side.

She informed me that she was a widow and that she had never been out with any other man except her husband, but friends had persuaded her to go dancing again. I asked if she would go out to lunch with me next time I was in town, and to my amazement, she said yes.

We went to a restaurant, but neither of us could eat any of our meal. She was a wee bit scared at doing something she never thought she could do, and I was a bit worried that I might put a foot wrong. But all went well, and I asked her whether she got out much. She explained that a few years ago she had contracted breast cancer, and she spent most of her time at home by herself. Subsequently I arranged to call on her on Saturday afternoons to take her out to various towns along the coast. She thoroughly enjoyed these days out.

On her birthday, I told her that I would cook a special meal, so she came over to my bungalow. How was I to know that she didn't like duck à l'orange? (Poor little duck!) We became constant companions after that, and one day she came back to my place to cook me cold beans on burnt toast (not my most favourite meal). She then went out to the conservatory to get some ice cream out of the freezer. I shouted out to her to mind the floor, as my cleaner had just washed it, and she had on high-heeled shoes. Too late! Crash she went on the floor. I gave her first aid and kept her warm in case of shock. Later, I took her to hospital, and the X-ray showed that she had broken her ankle. As she lived in a little terraced house, she asked if she could come over to my bungalow for six weeks until her plaster was taken off. That was about seven years ago, and I often asked her, wasn't her ankle better and wouldn't she like to return to Folkestone? The answer was always no.

This was no mad, passionate affair; it was just two very good friends living together in harmony. She was not a sexual lady (although very sexy), and this suited me because she would not go looking for greener pastures as most other ladies do. So here we were happily suited – best friends in the world. What more could a man want than to spend the rest of his life together in bliss with someone he worshipped? But I could never tell her.

We went out to lunch two or three times a week. We also went on shopping trips and to various seaside locations. We thoroughly enjoyed each other's company, twenty-four hours a day and seven days a week. She never wanted to go out in the evenings, preferring instead to see her soaps on television. She hated alcoholics and drunks, and so as not to upset her, I became a teetotaller. She had never been on a plane or a boat, and even though I obtained a passport for her, she had no inclination to go abroad, especially as she had a faithful old black Labrador named Leo as her constant companion. Unfortunately, two years ago, Leo died, as he was quite old, so I buried him in the back garden, adjacent to the marsh he loved to run on.

Just over a year ago, Lorna developed a continuous cough. The doctor said it was nothing to worry about and gave her antibiotics. Later she had a pain by her ribs and under her arm. The doctor said it was a trapped nerve, and he didn't even give her a painkiller. We changed her doctor, and he said the other doctor was probably right, but as she had had breast cancer, he would arrange for her to have a scan. After a three-month wait, she had the scan. The doctor asked her to attend his surgery and told her that she now had lung cancer.

To use his and her word, shit.

After a six-week wait, she saw a specialist who inserted a camera into her lung but found it clear. After a radioactive bone scan and a computer scan, where they put a probe through her back to take a biopsy, I began asking when she was going to get some remedial treatment. After another wait, she saw the doctor that had given her treatment for her breast cancer and in whom she had a lot of faith. He prescribed radiotherapy, and after a further three-week wait, it was given to her in two huge doses. By now she was experiencing a lot of pain, and she was prescribed morphine tablets. After radiotherapy, she was given steroids, indigestion tablets, and several other items to take.

Five weeks later, she had to return to see the specialist and have another X-ray taken. They said that they would contact the hospice; Lorna was terrified, as her husband had died in there. I told her that I was quite capable of looking after her and that I would bolt and barricade the door and wouldn't let them take her away. They did send down a very understanding nurse once a fortnight to check her medication and pain barrier. Lorna asked me to tell her the truth about her condition, but she didn't want to know how long she had to live. I told her the truth: that she had lung cancer and that it wouldn't go away by itself, but that I would look after her. She seemed satisfied by what I had told her, and we started going out to lunch, dancing, and shopping again, but she got very tired quickly and was glad to get back to her bed.

By this time, I was carrying phials of morphine around with me to keep her pain under control. Her steroids were causing her loss of sleep most of the night, and I had to purchase many women's books for her to read. I was also getting out of bed every few hours to make her cups of tea and to ensure that she was pain free. She then developed a pain in her hip. She had another radioactive bone scan, and they increased her morphine dosage; then she had another huge dose of radiotherapy on her hip and five more sessions of radiotherapy on her lung. After four sessions of this, she was quite exhausted.

One Sunday, she had difficulty in breathing, and I had to call the doctor out. He diagnosed a chest infection and called an ambulance, whereby she was taken to hospital. When the ambulance departed, he put his hand on my shoulder and said, "This is for the best, as we may be able to buy her a further couple of months. Also, it will give you a rest from looking after her."

I followed the ambulance as soon as I could and sat with her in A and E. Her sister, June, also turned up. All this time, she was on oxygen, and at about nine that evening, she was transferred to a ward.

Give me a rest? There I was, alone again in my bungalow.

Every day I drove up to the hospital and spent two or three hours with her, then I drove home again to wash her nightwear to take it up the following day. I couldn't sleep, didn't want to eat, had a continuous headache, and worried about how she was feeling. I would have preferred to have her here at home with me, as I didn't mind constantly taking her pills and cooking her things she liked to eat. As I said to her when she worried that it was unfair of her to stay in bed too long, at least the bungalow wasn't empty when I knew that she was in the bedroom, and that gave me a lot of comfort.

I went to the hospital and took the staff and patients some chocolates and Easter eggs, but poor Lorna had visibly deteriorated. As her right arm was useless, I fed her lunch (as I often had to). She was most upset that she was unable to speak to her sister when she phoned; she asked that I phone June and explain that she was better now.

Today she was most confused and didn't know what day it was; also she was obviously very heavily sedated. Lorna thought I looked distinguished in my glasses, and although I didn't have to wear them, I did so that she couldn't see my eyes. But I couldn't stop the tears from running down my cheeks, so I told her that I had a cold. The nurses told me that I should cry, otherwise I would make myself ill. I told them that big boys don't cry, but they said that they do. I should confide in neighbours, they said, but I didn't have any to confide in. They said I should see a doctor, but Lorna was the one who was ill, not me.

They told me subsequently that I had stayed at the hospital for thirty-six hours by her bedside, but I don't really remember that. She screamed out many times that she just wanted to die. I told her that I really should go home to get some sleep, shower, and change my clothes, but she constantly told me that I couldn't and that she wanted me to stay with her. Ultimately, I promised her that if she let me go home, I would return after a few hours' sleep and stay by her bedside again that night.

I'd had about three hours' sleep when the phone rang. It was the hospital; Lorna was asking for me again. I rapidly showered and got dressed, and I was off to the hospital as fast as possible. Her sister was there, and she moved over to let me sit and hold Lorna's hands. June then went off to get a cup of coffee.

Lorna's breathing was quite laboured, and her head was to one side, but I couldn't straighten it. She wanted to tell me something but didn't have any voice. I told her to go to sleep and tell me about it when she woke up. So I just sat holding her hands and kissing her cheek. After about twenty minutes, her breath failed, and she was dead. I went to see the nurse and told her that Lorna's spirit had left her body. It was 5.30 p.m. on Tuesday, 2 May.

Lorna had only been given to me to look after for seven short years. We were best friends. She was cremated and her ashes interred with those of her husband. Her name was inscribed on her husband's headstone. Now I was alone again.

Oh, Lorna, why did you have to die? We were so happy together.

Afterword

Living in Fulham, I had to take care of myself on the streets from a very early age; I also had to go to work. From the age of eight onwards, I had to fight to survive. Many of the lads, including myself, later went into the ring for the Young Britons and the Scouts, and several of my friends became professional afterwards.

So far, no mention has been made of the school that I went to. I passed the eleven-plus as a child of a poor working family, but my parents couldn't afford the cost of me going to a high school. Anyway, I don't think they had the slightest concern about which school I went to. I chose to go to a central school to learn French and bookkeeping. My mother could never get over the fact that she had to pay four shillings and sixpence for a school badge.

I got into the top stream of the school and won term prizes, and then, because my mum made me attend dancing lessons during the evenings so I could go on the stage, I was demoted to the lowest grade in front of the whole school because I hadn't done my homework. My dad used to tell me to tell the teachers that I did enough time during the day studying at school, and he wasn't going to spend his money on gaslight so that I could do homework. I still managed to come top of the class, though, and I still got prizes for the examinations. War broke out, and the school was evacuated, but as I stayed in London, my schooling ended when I was thirteen.

When I was a kid, my mother travelled all over to miss the Blitz on London, but at that time, I was working at J. Lyons in Hammersmith Road, so I couldn't always follow her. She went to my cousin's house in Isleworth. They hadn't been touched by the bombs, but then, after a few nights there, the Germans knocked seven bags of hell out of the place. After I joined the Navy, she went up to Smethick to avoid the raids, but the Germans found out about her movements and blew Smethick to bits. So we always said that the Germans knew where she was going and bombed accordingly.

I remember that in those days, there was a blackout, and all the windows were covered with sticky paper. On trains and buses they stuck net to all the windows, but people used to try peeling back the net to see where they were. In the end, the London Transport put notices by all their windows, saying, "I hope you'll pardon my correction, but that net is there for your protection."

All signposts and station names were taken away to prevent fifth columnists from finding out where they were.

At the end of the war, about two hundred matelots used to follow a submariner round Guz barracks, and they all cheered when the officers had to salute the submariner first. He got his VC by crawling through the bilges with a petty officer to defuse a time bomb that had been lodged there.

When I was on guard duty at Guz, I went round the barracks and heard loud shouting and hollering. I went into the mess deck, and there were about fifty of them all crowding round a table. The table was loaded with cigarettes, and one bright spark was measuring the length of the men's pinkies to see who had the longest, and then he with the longest took all the cigarettes.

On VJ Day, there was a riot in the chogi, and all the inmates ran round the top of the enclosing wall, with the regulating ratings trying to capture them. I understand that one leading seaman was stabbed in the stomach.

I remember being on leave in Smethwick and, at their father's insistence, escorting two sisters round Birmingham. I still remember the feeling I had, in the dark, fingering the whalebones in their corsets.

I did very well at work, rising from cleaner to engineer. I was successful at an interview and got a two-year training course to be a combustion engineer. I was teamed up with another young lad who had also been in combined ops but was full of himself.

Many of the men were extremely kind in those days. I was looking at an electrical diagram on the turbine floor one day when the operator said to me, "I'll show you how it all works. The steam comes along this pipe." It was an electrical diagram, so I coughed and said thank you.

I was walking along the boiler house floor one day when a stoker said, "'Ere, you want to know a bit about the fuel that we are burning?"

Dutifully I said yes, as I always appreciated learning more. He picked up a handful of coal from the hopper and said, "You know what we call this?" I was expecting him to say "scotch washed" or something like that, but he said, "We call that shit, mate."

That was what it was called. One learns something every day.

Many years passed, and I now lived near Maidstone. It was a location in the country, and I had built my wife some kennels. She was always away from home, and her mother would constantly be at our bungalow. One day, I arrived home from work to find her cooking a stew. I asked her where she had gotten the vegetables, and she said, "From the garden."

"Show me," I said.

It was just as well that I questioned her, because after she showed me, I found out that she had pulled out lily bulbs from the garden to use as onions.

I love my daughter very deeply and see her and her family now about four times a year. They come down to see me with the rest of her family.

When her mother left home, my daughter was very upset, and she locked herself in her room. I used to come home from work, cook her food, and leave it outside her door. After about four months, she said that her mother had contacted her and would take her to the USA on holiday. I was very pleased about that because I had to give my ex-wife a pension, a lump sum, and a house and car, and I knew that she had the cash to spare.

Later my daughter came back to me and said, "Dad, Mother expects me to pay my own way."

I knew that she didn't have the cash, so I gave her the money to pay. She didn't let my contribution go unrewarded; she brought me back a bottle of whisky, but she had put it in her case for safekeeping. The bottle got smashed, and all her clothes and the contents in the case stank of whisky.

My middle son obtained a degree from the London School of Economics and then travelled round India for two years. I hadn't seen him in over twenty-eight years, but he came back on holiday a couple of weeks ago from Thailand, where he lives and works. I was very pleased to see him and told him not to leave it so long next time. I told him to come back in twenty-seven years, as he said he would like to visit me again.

The youngest son also came back home from Jersey, where he is a coach driver, but he likes his booze. He stayed on the wagon all the time he was here, and I was very pleased to see him.

Conclusions

I am now approaching my middle eighties, but I tell everyone that I am fifty next week. I met a woman round the corner and told her that I was fifty next week. She said, "Wait until you reach my age."

To which I replied, "How old are you, then?"

She said, "I am sixty-two."

"My goodness!" I replied. "I didn't know that one could last that long."

I guess I am really lucky in that I don't look my age, but I still love to laugh, and I constantly joke about things. One way to keep looking young is to keep one's mind occupied; I do this by using the Internet. I send round jokes every day to many people because one must remember that there are many people confined to their homes who cannot get out, so they use the Internet to keep in touch with other people. Now, many people send jokes to me to circulate, so I am the first to see many of them. Never clock-watch or say that you are bored and want time to go faster because later in life, you will treasure every moment, and you will find that one never has the time to do all the things that one wants to do.

Another way of keeping the mind active is to have a few hobbies. I buy a few shares on the stock market, but I wouldn't expect other people to do the same, as it's a very risky place to make a few bob. I have been doing it for over forty years, and I could still lose a fortune.

I collected postcards. Having assembled a collection of "One Hundred Years of War and Peace," I used to lecture at various clubs. I also collected "Prisoner of War Post," and lots of people used to like looking at those, and they listened intently to what I had to say about prison camps during wartime.

I am also the only teetotaller to run a pub on the Internet, and people come from far and wide to have their say. In fact, I do anything that keeps my mind active. All in all, I have lived a very happy life. I've had many laughs, although I have had a few sad spots. I thought that I would tell everyone about them, and I hope that I have made you laugh and cry with some of my thoughts, be they fact or fiction.

I have now moved to the seaside, and with the sea in front of the house and the marsh just behind, it's where I want to be. It's also very isolated, with just a few houses nearby. I have lived here for over thirty years, and I love it. I wouldn't move anywhere else.

I met Daphne in a local café six years ago, and she now lives in my bungalow. We get on very well, and as her husband died of cancer about eight years ago, she also understands what I had to go through with Lorna.

I still manage to drive short distances, to lunch and shopping about four or five times a week, but now I have to wear glasses (but they don't hold enough beer). We love Wednesdays because that is the day we go to another town for our fish and chips and to do our shopping. I'm not going anywhere, so you will still be bothered by me for a while yet.

I've had two heart attacks, and Saint Peter said to me, "Are you ready to come with me?"

I said, "Yes, I'll just collect a few things."

He said, "Oh, no, you can't take any earthly possessions with you."

I replied, "Then I'm not going."

At the end of the war, I applied for my medals, but they said that my papers had been lost. I was given ten points off my demobbed number (for hazardous duties). Recently, I made further application to the medal office, but they told me that my papers were still lost. (Well, they would, wouldn't they?) I told them some of the things that I had been up to, but they said that combined operations was like the secret service and never divulged what its members had been up to, so the only medal that was available to me was the War Medal, or Victory

Medal, as we knew it. Yet I was told off during the war for not wearing the '39–'45 star. If I wanted to apply for the defence medal, I would have to apply to a different location. As far as I am concerned, I shan't bother.

I can't walk very far now. I can run as fast as a young person can walk, but I keep falling over. When you next see an older person, don't brush him aside. If you talk to him, you may be amazed because he has had a very interesting life and done things that you never would. Well, Daphne's mum is one hundred and one and still alive and kicking, so I've still got a lot of living to do. Excuse me if I hurry away, as I'm a very busy person.

Glossary of Terms

- A and E = accident and emergency
- ack-ack battalion = anti-aircraft battalion
- ARP = Air Raid Precaution
- bevvies = drinks
- the Blitz = air raid
- bloater = smoked herring
- boffin = inventor
- Brahms and Liszt = drunk
- café = tea or coffee house
- chogi = naval prison
- Civvy Street = civilian
- clippie = bus conductress
- crashed our swedes = slept
- demobbed = demobilised; released from the forces
- E-boat = German motor torpedo boat
- Fyffes = brand of bananas

- Guz = Devonport

- GP = general practitioner, or doctor

- HMS = His Majesty's Ship

- hooky = leading seaman

- jemmy = iron bar (used for opening things)

- Kate Carnie's army (combined operations) = comical description of army

- kedge = anchor

- killick = leading seaman

- kye = chocolate drink

- M coil = thirty turns of cable round the ship to demagnetize it.

- megger = continuity tester

- nissed as a pewt = drunk

- Ogin = sea

- oppo = friend

- penny = one twelfth of a shilling

- RAF = Royal Air Force

- RAMC = Royal Army Medical Corps

- REME = Royal Electrical and Mechanical Engineers

- rozzer = copper or policeman

- shite hawks = sea gulls

- sit-upon = back passage

- the Smoke = London

- South Coast = southern part of England on the coast

- squaddy = soldier

- square bashing = marching and drill

- sub-station = high voltage switching station

- tickler = handmade cigarettes

- tiffies = medical staff

- titfer = hat or cap

- tot = daily ration of rum

- trot boat = a boat that collects servicemen from their craft

- the Underground = tube railway, mainly in London

- West End = the area populated with cinemas and restaurants in London

- Wren (WRNS) = Women's Royal Naval Service

- yomp = thirty-mile run with full kit